I0582474

THE WRIGHT DETECTIVE

THE WRIGHT DETECTIVE

Book Three:
A Haunting in Greeneville

Kelly Swan Taylor

Published by Link Press

Providence, Rhode Island

The Wright Detective #3 – First edition
Copyright © 2022 by Kelly Swan Taylor

Cover design and illustration by Michael Borkowski
Interior images by Jonathan M. Taylor

Library of Congress Control Number: 2022919197
ISBN: (paperback) 978-1-7376244-8-6
ISBN: (ebook) 978-1-7376244-7-9
IBG 1.24-1026

For my readers—
Whether as kids or kids-at-heart, together we
are bridging the gap.

For little girls who aren't satisfied with being
princesses—
Let us always strive to be queens.

Chapter 1

Closing her worn hardcover edition of *Little Women*, Tessa leaned back into her beanbag chair. "Summer reading's officially done!" she declared, raising her arms in a "V" for victory toward her treehouse ceiling. With her eighth-grade year at Greeneville Heights Middle starting in only a couple of days, this was the latest she'd ever finished a summer reading assignment. Usually, she was done before the Fourth of July. But this summer had been filled with distractions. The most recent one made her stomach swarm with butterflies: her new *boyfriend* Mason. Then, her mind shifted to her impressive triumph in solving the case of the missing championship basketball trophy.

Tessa ran her fingertips over the antique cover of her novel. It had been her grandmother Theresa's favorite in her vast reading collection. She was now living in Florida and tending to her garden while sending jars and jars of homemade jam. Tessa missed her and her late grandfather, Cameron. With a sigh, she gingerly placed the novel into her book bin. She was reaching for her next *Nancy Drew* novel in the series when there was commotion below. "Tessa! Pizza's here!" her three best friends shouted in unison.

Glancing at her Garmin running watch, Tessa shook her head in disbelief. Had she been reading all morning long? It was now time for her usual Sunday afternoon meeting of the TSLR Detective Agency and she hadn't even prepared for it. She really was distracted. "Um, come on up!"

A pizza box was the first thing to peek up from the ladder, followed by Leah, treasurer extraordinaire. "Last meeting of the summer!" she cheered.

"Why are you so chipper about it?" Skylar asked behind her. The VP rolled her eyes and pushed back her long, blonde hair. "This totally sucks."

Riley was last to arrive, diligently opening her secretary's notebook before she even sat down. "I think this year is gonna be great. Eighth grade and starting cross-country. Right, Tessa?" Track stars Tessa and Riley had recently ventured into another sport, and their first meet was already coming up fast.

"Um, yeah," Tessa said, fumbling with her notes at the table she used as her president's podium. Her normally organized green agency binder was a horrible mess, with papers sticking out everywhere.

Skylar reached into the pizza box for a slice, then handed it to Leah. "Whatever, Riley. We know you just want to see your new *boyfriend* Nick at practice!"

As she looked up from her notebook, Riley's cheeks turned scarlet from behind her glasses. "He's not my boyfriend. Nick is just a friend." She lowered her head back to her notebook, but her face continued to redden.

The minutes ticked by while the girls chatted, passed around the pizza box, and handed out sodas, until finally,

Skylar focused on their flustered president. "Tessa, what on earth are you looking for up there?"

Three sets of curious eyes moved to Tessa as silence filled the space. "I can't find my—"

"Here it is!" Leah said, pulling the wooden gavel from under her orange floor pillow.

Tessa groaned, taking the gavel. "Thanks." *How the heck did it get there?*

"Are you okay, Tessa?" Riley asked, her pencil poised to start recording the meeting minutes.

She threw up her hands. "Sorry, guys. I was so busy finishing the summer reading, I totally forgot about the meeting. Just … distracted lately."

"Well, with such a cute boyfriend, Tessa, it's totally understandable," Skylar said between bites of crust.

"Agreed," said Leah, waving a tempting pizza slice in Tessa's periphery. "Let's forget about the meeting and relax on our last weekend before school starts."

Skylar perked up. "Love that idea! What do we have for cases anyway?"

Tessa turned to the bulletin board behind her. At least *that* was organized. "Not too much, honestly. Some missing items, as usual. I think things are slow because no one is going out."

"I know. Downtown is more like a *ghost town* with all the break-ins," Leah said. Over the past few months, Greeneville Heights' bustling business district had been hit with so many break-ins that everyone was spooked.

"Any updates from your dad, Tessa?" Riley asked.

Tessa's dad, retired Marine Drew Wright, was the lead detective on the Greeneville police force. He had been getting pressured for years to take on the job of Chief of Police. And now that Chief Woodbridge was ready to retire, everyone knew it was pretty much a done deal. That is, if he could stop the crime wave.

Giving up on the official meeting, Tessa flopped down beside her friends. "I thought he had a lead when they found those bike tracks at Carmichael's. But it's hard to investigate disappearing evidence."

"Wow. Ghost town. Disappearing evidence. Maybe it's paranormal," Skylar joked.

Ignoring her, Leah asked, "Tessa, did you really see a Dunbar Deliveries sign at the scene?"

Biting into her pizza, Tessa sighed. "I'm pretty positive I wouldn't have imagined it. But when I tried to tell my dad, it seemed ridiculous. I'm gonna try to bring it up again tonight when he gets home from work."

Leah tapped her financial ledger with her drawing pencil. "If we solve a case of this magnitude, we definitely should get a huge donation from the city, right? Perfect for our treehouse improvements." The room collectively rolled its eyes. Leah was still trying to gain support for her idea of using agency funds, donated from successful cases, to add a flat-screen and HVAC system to the treehouse.

Suddenly, Skylar dropped her pizza crust on the floor. "I don't know how I forgot to tell you guys! I totally got some wild intel from Caleb. Actually, it's inside info from Ethan." Caleb was Skylar's older-by-eight-minutes twin brother and his best friend, Ethan, was her ex-boyfriend. "It's about Willow Roberts."

Tessa almost choked on her soda. Willow was an annoyance in everyone's life, especially since she decided to move from Avondale to Greeneville Heights. She was pretty on the outside, but not on the inside. And she was now dating Ethan. "Willow? I'm afraid to ask," Tessa managed as the soda burned down her throat and through her nostrils.

Skylar hunched forward like she was about to reveal a compelling secret. "So, apparently, her parents bought that old, creepy house on Waverly. You know, the Huntington Manor."

A few *gasps* circulated among the tree limbs, and Tessa felt herself involuntarily shiver, even in the summer heat. Riley dropped her notebook and wrapped her arms around her knees. "That house has been deserted for years. How can they possibly move in there?"

"I know. It's gotta be like Miss Havisham's cobweb palace in *Great Expectations*," Tessa said with a grimace.

"Totally," Skylar agreed. "But I guess they're fixing it up."

Leah started collecting the trash around the treehouse. "They could fix that place up like Buckingham Palace and it still won't purge all those ghosts."

"Anyway, I guess they're moving in soon. So, we'll see how brave Willow is sleeping under that roof," Skylar said, standing and wiping crumbs off her shorts. "I gotta get going. Piano lesson in a few."

Everyone nodded, knowing Skylar was done for the day. She'd become the new piano protégé of her teacher, rocker Justin. They were now good friends, and Skylar had developed a newfound love of music.

"Thanks for stopping by, guys. Sorry about the ... mess," Tessa said, pointing to the still-disheveled table of agency paperwork.

"No biggie. We'll get back at it next week," Leah said, hugging her president.

When Skylar and Leah had disappeared down the treehouse ladder, Riley remained and handed Tessa a sheet of paper from her notebook. "What's this?" Tessa asked.

Looking sheepish, she said, "Just notes from today. I couldn't help it."

They laughed as Tessa reread the fun banter of their non-meeting. Lifting her eyes from the paper, she said, "So, really. What is going on with you and Nick? You guys can't stay away from each other at cross-country practice."

Riley's gaze moved to her feet. "It doesn't matter if we like each other because my parents won't let me date. Not until I'm sixteen anyway."

Tessa did a double take. Sure, they were only thirteen, but it wasn't like they were eloping. With Mason, the two might go to the movies or grab an innocent burger at the local diner. "Really? You never mentioned that before."

Groaning, Riley clutched her notebook to her chest. "I guess they didn't feel the need to share that I couldn't date until, you know, I actually *wanted* to."

"I'm sorry, Riley." Then, something occurred to her. "Hey, how about you two come out with Mason and me some-time? It's more of a group hangout than—"

"A double date," Riley said, smiling.

"Exactly."

Riley was so excited, she was practically swinging from the rafters of the treehouse. "Okay. Since you helped me, how about I help you?"

Tessa tossed her a confused look until Riley pointed to the mess on the table. "Yes, please. At this rate, I'll be here until we start school in a couple of days."

"No problem, bestie."

Chapter 2

Early the next morning, Tessa was jolted awake by the piercing scream of her baby brother, Cam. Practically leaping out of her comfy sleigh bed, she rubbed her eyes and blinked away her sleepiness. With a glance at the clock, she groaned. "Six o'clock? Seriously?" She couldn't even sleep in on the last day before the new school year started!

Tessa was about to flip over and cover her ears with a pillow when she heard a tap on her door. "Come in," she moaned.

Her mom peeked her head inside. "I'm sorry, sweetie. Hanna will be here any minute. Cam is running a bit of a fever."

Propelling herself upright, Tessa was now much more alert. As much as she'd disliked the idea of her new surprise sibling from the very beginning, he was her brother after all. "Is he okay?"

Tessa's mom took a seat on the edge of her bed. Wearing her usual attire of scrubs, she appeared bright-eyed and ready to attend to her pediatric patients at her downtown practice. "Just a slightly elevated temperature with a little cold. Nothing to worry about. But it does make him cranky." Leaning forward, she pushed Tessa's chestnut pixie cut out of her sapphire eyes. "It's getting long again. Maybe another visit to Sue Ann's soon?"

"I was wondering if I should let it grow out a bit. With fall coming."

Dr. Wright looked taken aback. Tessa had loved her short hair, especially with all the running she did in the heat of the South. "Really? What brought this on?"

Tessa shrugged. "I don't know. Something I've been debating. Not sure yet."

Studying her daughter for a beat, Dr. Wright said, "Well, I'm sure Mason will like it short or long."

"Mom, I'm not choosing my hairstyle because of a boy," she said, scoffing at her mom's comment. "It's my choice. If he doesn't like it—too bad." Of course, Mason wasn't so shallow to think he could suggest to Tessa what to do with her hair. But she knew he would probably like it either way.

Dr. Wright chuckled and pulled her into a hug. "You are definitely my daughter." When the room shook from the slam of the front door, she said, "Our savior is here. Get some rest, and I'll have Hanna make your favorite breakfast." Tessa smiled, already mentally drooling over a plate of French toast and strawberries with piping-hot syrup. Hanna (their housekeeper and nanny) knew the perfect amount of cinnamon to add to the recipe and always delivered her masterpiece with a beaming grin.

Three hours later, Tessa stumbled out of bed wondering how she was ever going to get back to a normal school schedule. Especially in only one day. After a long, soothing shower, she was still yawning while heading downstairs to the kitchen. The second her nose caught the delicious sweet and spicy aroma of cinnamon, she was wide-awake.

"Tessa, my dear. Good morning," their Slovak housekeeper said cheerfully from the stainless range. Her blue paisley apron was freshly ironed and tied with an impeccable bow. Armed with a spatula and her gray hair styled into a bun, she hummed as Tessa's orange tabby kitten roamed in a tight circle around her feet.

"Sorry about Sherlock, Hanna." Tessa waved a rattling mouse toy at the kitten to grab his attention before snagging a stool at the marble island.

Hanna left the stove and placed a scrumptious plate in front of Tessa. "Oh, he's no bother. Keeps me company while I'm tidying up."

Scanning the kitchen for another furry friend, Tessa asked, "Where's Watson?" Sherlock's buddy was, in fact, Riley's little kitten. But her parents, still working out the dynamics of their divorce, simply didn't think a pet fit into that scenario. Both Tessa and her best friend hoped that would soon change. In the meantime, Watson was a member of the Wright family.

"He was napping on the patio earlier, getting some morning sun. He's certainly more mellow than this ginger cutie here."

"That's for sure." Tessa pointed to Sherlock, who was currently chasing speckles of sunlight seeping through the back windows.

Hanna patted Tessa affectionately on the shoulder. "So, what wonderful plans do you have for your last morning of summer vacation? I hope it isn't all schoolwork."

Tessa would have groaned, but she checked her watch and remembered exactly what she was doing in a few hours.

"Actually, I finished my summer reading yesterday with *Little Women*. Today is all about fun."

"Ah. That is such a lovely tale. Four close sisters. Reminds you of your friends, no?"

Reaching for the hot syrup pitcher, Tessa gave it a thought. "Yeah. I guess it does. We're all different but still get along." She tapped her chin and nodded to herself. "That's a good idea, Hanna."

The cheerful housekeeper slid a glass of freshly squeezed orange juice over to Tessa. "What's a good idea?"

"We're supposed to pick one book from our summer reading list to write a little essay about. Just how it compares with our life. Very open-ended. It's not due for a couple of weeks, but now I have a topic, thanks to you."

Beaming, Hanna dropped crunchy kibble into Sherlock's bowl. "Happy to help, my dear. Although, with your inquisitive mind, I'm sure you would have come up with it yourself."

While Tessa ate her breakfast, the two brainstormed the details of her essay and discussed the upcoming school year. Hanna really was becoming a cherished member of the family. "I can help with the dishes," Tessa offered, carrying her plate to the sink.

"Oh, no, my dear. Thank you for offering, but it is such a beautiful day, and don't you have preparations to make for … later?"

Tessa smacked her hand to her forehead. "You're right. I have a ton of wrapping to get perfect."

"Well, the cupcakes should be ready in plenty of time to frost them. Do you need anything else?" Hanna's eyes grew bright. "How about sparkling cider? That's celebratory, no?"

Now, giddy with excitement, Tessa hugged her sweet, endearing housekeeper. "Another great idea, Hanna!"

Her face showed delight. "I'm so glad. Now, go and enjoy this gorgeous day."

A couple of hours later, Tessa raced to her treehouse with full hands. She was such a mixture of excitement and nervousness that she nearly dropped her armful onto her dad's pristine golf-course-esque lawn. "At least I didn't drop everything in the pool," she said to herself, thinking a nice dip would be a great way to end the summer. But there simply wasn't time.

She blew out a sigh of relief when she'd successfully hauled everything up the precarious rungs of her treehouse. Wiping beads of perspiration off her forehead, she centered the cupcakes on the table as well as the chilled bottle of sparkling cider with fancy glasses Hanna provided. To add to the festive feel, Tessa hung evergreen and white balloons all over the perimeter of the room and draped streamers across the ceiling. All around her, the past couple of hours of hard work shined. And she knew it would be appreciated.

Tessa was still tweaking the streamer placement when the treehouse ladder creaked loudly. Her heart skipped a beat as she scooped up the packages from the table. Trembling with nervous excitement, she hoped she wouldn't drop them—especially when she heard, "Hey, Tessa!" from below.

She sucked in a deep, calming breath and answered, "Come on up!"

Grinning from ear to ear, Tessa clutched the packages tightly as Mason's dark, wavy hair popped up from the ladder. "Wow," he said with both his mouth and his exquisite emerald eyes as he stepped inside.

"Happy birthday, Mason Greene!" Tessa shouted.

Chapter 3

For a moment, Mason seemed to be at a loss for words. His eyes moved around the room but delightfully landed on Tessa, her tiny frame virtually hidden behind the packages. "Wow," he repeated, approaching her. "I mean, wow!"

"Too much?" she joked but was still anxious that it was somewhat true. Even though he had asked her to the spring dance months ago, they'd only been officially dating for a few weeks. Maybe this was a little over-the-top.

She gnawed on her bottom lip as Mason walked up to her and the packages. "Are all these for me?"

"Unless you know of another guy with a birthday today. In that case, you have to share."

Mason chuckled at her sarcasm. With raised eyebrows, he took the gifts from her arms. "Thank you, Tessa." She was surprised when he set them on the table and pulled her into a hug. "And thank you for all of this. It's perfect."

Tingles moved up Tessa's spine being so close to him. This was happening more lately. Mason had started as a friend, progressed to an even better friend, and recently asked her to be his *girlfriend*. Tessa was still in shock and having trouble saying the word. But when she did, she couldn't help but smile. "You're so welcome, Mason."

When he pulled away, he gently held on to her arms. "I used to hate having a birthday right before school started, but this might change my mind."

As their eyes held for what seemed like forever, Tessa wondered if he was going to kiss her—as in, a *real* kiss (of the non-cheek variety). She involuntarily shivered at the thought. His eyes wavered over her lips as his grin widened. *What's he thinking?* Sadly, her telekinetic powers really only worked with Riley.

"Shall we have a toast?" he eventually asked, reaching forward but only for the glasses.

"Um, sure," she said, slightly disappointed. He opened the bottle, poured them each a glass, and handed one to her. "To you and your birthday ..." she started.

"How about to *both* of us? To my birthday and all this *amazingness* you did." Then, he pulled an adorable face. "I totally just made up that word. I clearly couldn't come up with one to describe this."

Giggling, Tessa clinked their glasses. "You're the cutest, Mason Greene." Then, she bit her lip. It just came out. As she gulped down her cider, heat moved up her cheeks.

Mason took a sip from his glass, then gave her an appley kiss on the cheek. "Back at you," he whispered.

The treehouse was getting ridiculously warm, only partially from the afternoon heat. "How about you open your presents?" Tessa asked, needing a distraction.

"You don't have to ask me twice. I love presents!"

She guided him over to the beanbag chair she'd moved to the middle of the room and carried the packages to him.

There was one large box on the bottom, topped with a smaller package, all wrapped meticulously in iridescent dark green paper. A shimmering white bow was on top, securing an envelope. "I love the Greeneville Middle color theme. Everything matches," he said, pointing around the room.

Shrugging, she sat beside him on a floor cushion. "I couldn't resist."

"So, what should I open first?"

Tessa considered his question. "How about the big one on the bottom?"

He slowly started unwrapping the taped edges as she anxiously watched. When he continued to carefully remove tape at a snail's pace, Tessa made a face. "That seriously is the strangest gift unwrapping I've ever seen. You're supposed to rip it open like a five-year-old."

Mason laughed. "Sorry. I always do it like this. My mom never liked the mess. Plus, you did such an awesome wrap job." When he finally finished, he gently set the paper down on the floor. Tessa could barely contain her excitement as he lifted the box's top and sifted through the tissue paper. "Oh, wow," he gushed, and pulled the heavy evergreen hoodie out of the box. In white lettering was written "Greeneville Heights Middle School Falcons," with an image of a basketball. But when he saw the top left sleeve, he gasped. "Captain" was spelled out in white. "Tessa, this is … awesome!"

"Flip it over," she said, shaking with nervousness.

He did as she instructed and let out another *gasp*. On the back of the sweatshirt was printed "Greene" on top with the number "44" in large white print in the center. For the past couple of seasons, Mason was a shooting guard and proudly wore the number "14." But, after his awe-inspiring performance on the team all season and as MVP at the championship game, he was not only voted as team captain but was moved up to point guard. The number he chose was "44."

"I don't know what to say," he whispered at last, his eyes never leaving the sweatshirt.

Leaning in, Tessa said, "I asked Caleb what to get you, and he said that the team wanted to bling out your official sweatshirt, like this. So, I offered to have it made. Skylar came with me. Do you know that Cleo now does screen printing?" Tessa had gotten her dress for the dance at Cleo's dress shop. She was an incredible designer, who had just the right thing for Tessa's petite frame. When Mason remained quiet, she said, "Well, try it on."

It was a perfect fit and complemented his eyes so well that Tessa couldn't stop staring. Her breath hitched when he scooped her up from the floor pillow and pulled her into the beanbag chair for a hug of soft cotton. "This is the best gift, Tessa. Thank you."

As they faced each other in the chair, their eyes once again held. "Um, you have another one." She pointed to the smaller gift, and he put his arm around her before grabbing it off the floor. He snuggled close to her and ripped the paper off in one swift motion. "Ah, you're learning," she teased.

In Mason's lap sat a nice hardcover edition of the *A Wrinkle in Time* series. He lifted the heavy book and the cover shimmered blue. Inside, the pages were lined in gold. The elaborate illustration on front was the crowning jewel. "Geez, Tessa. This is amazing too."

"Well, you really loved the first one. I guess there are more books in the series."

"I don't know what to say. These are so thoughtful, Tessa."

Without thinking, she rested her head on his shoulder. "You still have the card."

Taking his gaze off his book, he lifted the envelope. "Do you have a letter opener?"

Tessa raised her head. "For real?"

"I wanna keep the envelope too," he said sheepishly. Chuckling, Tessa crawled to Leah's art bin and found something that would work. He sliced the envelope open and revealed a handmade card in the same green and white with a birthday cake and candles. Written across the front was *Happy 14th Birthday, Mason!*

"You're lucky," she said, "I have to wait until the spring to see that number."

He laughed. "Yeah. Strange September birthdays." Inspecting the card in the light, he asked, "Did you make this?"

"Yeah. Leah helped. Apparently, I can't cut straight to save my life."

"It's way better than my clip art." With another laugh, he opened the card:

Mason,
Wishing you the best day ever! Thank you for asking me to the spring dance and for being such a great friend. Love, Tessa.

"Wow," he said for the umpteenth time. When he lifted his eyes from the card, they were sincere. "Thank you for saying 'yes.' Twice, actually." Tessa blushed, knowing he also meant when he asked her to be his girlfriend.

They were quiet for several beats, sitting close in the beanbag chair. Tessa could feel her heart pounding and hoped he couldn't detect it. "Um, do you want a cupcake? Hanna made them," she said softly.

"Oh. Sure. They look delicious."

The two enjoyed Hanna's latest masterpiece of yellow cake and chocolate frosting. It was Tessa's favorite, but she quickly discovered that it was Mason's as well. "What do you think?" Tessa asked, a few mouthfuls in.

"I think you'd better watch out because Hanna might leave you to open her own bakery. This is the best cupcake I've ever had." Then, Mason scanned the treehouse. "I still can't believe you let me in here." So far, Mason had been the only boy allowed in the treehouse after years of "Girls Only." And he was even voted in as an official member of the agency. But he preferred to let the girls have their meetings to themselves.

"Are you excited about your party?" she asked. Mason had decided to delay his official birthday party at the local bowling alley because of the new school year starting. And, he knew Tessa had her first cross-country meet coming up that Saturday.

Eyeing the festive scene around the treehouse, he said, "Yeah. But Greeneville Lanes can't possibly compete with all of this in a couple of weeks."

"So, it was a good surprise?"

Mason gave her another kiss on the cheek. "The best, Tessa."

A little later, when Tessa was cleaning up, Mason picked up his perfectly unwrapped paper, folded it, and pocketed it. "What's that for?" she asked.

Giving her a coy grin, he said, "I want to keep it. To remind me of today."

As butterflies fluttered in her stomach, Tessa knew she'd never forget it.

Chapter 4

"Yes! We're finally eighth-graders!" Skylar cheered as she and Tessa biked to school the next morning. She raced down the tallest hill a few blocks from the red brick building as Tessa lagged. "Aren't you excited?" she asked over her shoulder.

"Yeah. Got a lot on my mind, I guess." Despite getting a decent night of sleep, Tessa woke up anxious for both the new year in general and one with Mason. She'd never had a boyfriend before. How was she even supposed to act around him at school?

Skylar slowed to a crawl. "Why so melancholy? You had a great day with Mason yesterday, right?"

"Yeah. It's just . . ." Tessa leaned forward to whisper. "I kept thinking he was going to kiss me, and he didn't. Like a *real* kiss."

Scoffing, Skylar said, "That's easy. Just kiss him."

Tessa stopped pedaling and stared at her friend with her mouth agape. "Are you kidding?"

"No. What's wrong with taking the lead?"

Playing with her hands, Tessa mumbled, "Because I've never kissed anyone before."

Relaxing over her handlebars, Skylar studied her. "So? What does that matter?"

Tessa groaned, tilting her head back to the pale blue sky, streaked cotton-candy pink with early-morning clouds. "It matters because I have no idea what I'm doing. I have no idea what I am doing with any of this." Her eyes floated down to the ground. "You always seemed to know with Ethan."

"Well, super sleuth, you're wrong about that. Clearly, I had no idea who I was dating. And you know we never kissed. Not because I didn't want to, but because I was waiting for him. Guys are even more clueless."

Tessa knew that Mason had chickened out with holding her hand at the movies. He admitted it. But weren't they good enough friends to talk about this stuff? It seemed so silly to just guess. Then again, it was so awkward. "What do I do at school, then, Sky? And today? Our schedules say we share first period." *English again!*

Skylar rubbed her chin. "Why not ask him to hold your hand—better yet, take his—and have him walk you to class? That's way *adorbs.*"

"Okay," Tessa said, nodding. "That's a good plan. But what about the kissing thing? I don't even know how."

"And you think Mason does?"

She contemplated this for a beat. "Well, he's really cute. Girls at school like him."

"Yeah. But this is Mason Greene, Tessa. The guy is the most polite, sweet dude on the planet. I honestly wouldn't be surprised if he asked permission to kiss you, with like a slip of paper and stuff."

Letting out a burst of laughter, Tessa remounted her bike. "That does sound like him. Which is nice. But I kinda like the idea of a spontaneous moment. You know, when romance strikes him."

As they started off down the next hill, Skylar shook her head. "Who would have thought, logical, master brain Tessa would be more of a romantic than the rest of us?"

Tessa was surprised herself. Up until the moment when Mason asked her to the dance, she'd sworn off boys, especially in the treehouse and agency. And certainly, her brother's arrival didn't help. But everything seemed different now. Maybe it wasn't about *a* boy, but *the right* one.

The schoolyard was packed and buzzing when the girls rolled in. They parked their bikes in the rack beside a hefty oak with a massive canopy of green leaves, their edges barely tinged with orange. Tessa took a visual tour of the campus and smiled. All three Greeneville Heights schools (elementary, middle, and high) were clustered together and surrounded by large shade trees and sprawling green sports fields. But this red brick building had been her home for the past two years. She blew out a sigh at the thought of heading just next door to the even more impressive high school complex next year.

"Oh, look! There's Leah," Skylar said, pointing to a boisterous group of eighth-graders. "Yuck. There's my brother." She rolled her eyes and waved Tessa to follow. Leah and Caleb had been hanging out a lot. But, as far as anyone could tell, including Leah, Caleb was still too immature to be more than a friend. And at that very moment, he was goofing around so annoyingly with his fellow basketball teammates, it was obvious that none of that had changed over the summer.

Then, Tessa noticed Mason was also in the circle, his emerald eyes framed by his (equally as impressive) long eyelashes. Her heart skipped around a little, and she was now aware of how sweaty her palms were. Definitely not hand-holding-worthy. She wiped them off on her new denim skirt and adjusted her lightweight backpack. At least that was one benefit of the first day of school—empty binders and no textbooks.

Tessa was about to join the group when Rocky Redmond rolled to a halt right in front of her and flipped his scenic Hawaiian-themed skateboard with graceful finesse. "Hey, Tessa. Thanks again for finding my board this summer."

The way he was cradling the skateboard in his arms made her chest swell with pride. She loved that the agency could do such simple but important things for the community she loved. "No problem, Rocky. We were happy to help."

He popped the bubble he was making with his gum and leaned into her ear. "Did you really chase down Rex Jamison in the park, like in those action movies? People keep telling me stories all over town."

Tessa was taken aback. *People?* "Oh. I guess, yeah. So, you know the guy who took it?"

Rocky dropped his board onto the ground with another bubble pop. "Yup. Rex is a major jerk. Should stay in Westgate where he belongs. He's even known for taking little kids' bikes and scooters." Rocky shook his head as he mounted his board atop several palm trees and flew down the sidewalk. "Thanks again, Tessa!"

"Another happy customer?"

Tessa turned and virtually jumped out of her skin seeing Mason beside her. She was so taken off guard, she couldn't seem to form words. He looked adorable in shorts and an evergreen basketball t-shirt. Tessa couldn't wait to see him wearing his new sweatshirt, once fall really arrived and the southern temps went below blazing.

"Um, yeah. Rocky has been so appreciative."

Mason angled forward, his hands placed securely on his backpack straps. "Well, I don't blame him. I was there, remember? You must have clocked a four-minute mile keeping up with the thief on that skateboard!"

She couldn't help but laugh. Poor Mason practically collapsed after the chase. "Thanks," she said, wiping her hands on her skirt again. *Why's he so cute when he smiles?*

"You wanna head inside? I'm already sweating out of this t-shirt." Tessa didn't see that at all. Mason looked fresh as a daisy. She was the one with the dripping palms and was relieved when he kept his hands on his backpack.

As they walked beside each other, it was apparent how much taller he'd gotten over the summer. She secretly envied him, as that never seemed to happen to her.

"Hey! Here's the adorable couple now!" Caleb shouted at them from several yards away. Heat crept up Tessa's neck. While everyone knew she and Mason went to the dance together and even hung out over the summer, only their close friends knew they were an official couple.

Leah bounded in from the group to rescue her, hooking her arm around Tessa and steering her away. "Sorry. He seriously has no self-control. Skylar punched him like five times already."

"It's okay. People will get wind soon anyway," Tessa said softly.

"Why don't you two go ahead of us?" she said to the couple. Then, she added to Tessa, "I'll rein in the zoo with a distraction." Leah ran back to the circle and started teasing Caleb so badly that everyone couldn't take their eyes off the scene. It was masterful.

Mason even seemed intrigued until Tessa reached for his hand and pulled him forward. He was snapped back to attention and followed her inside into the whirl of refreshing air-conditioning. It absolutely gave a new meaning to *keep her cool.*

As they wandered into the bright, gleaming space that screamed spirited evergreen from floor to ceiling and was adorned with their fierce Falcon mascot, Tessa felt at home. She couldn't help but think of her last successful case at the agency. "Hey, let's go visit the trophy."

"Good idea."

When they stepped up to the massive glass case, Tessa's gaze immediately moved to her track team's two gilded gems, sitting side by side. *Two-time State Champions!* But she was especially proud of the recently recovered State Championship basketball trophy and gleefully pointed to the award topped with a large gold basketball. "No longer an empty spot."

Mason wrapped his arm around her. "Thanks to you." Tessa shrugged, but inside, she was beaming. "Speaking of cases, how's your dad doing with the break-ins? I heard another place got hit last weekend."

"Yeah. It was some small convenience store on the edge of town, near Westgate. No security cameras either."

"Does your dad still suspect it's an inside job? Seems pretty spread out."

Tessa sighed. "Yeah. Another with no sign of an actual break-in. I swear we must have a thief with superpowers or really great lock-picking skills."

Mason chuckled, the corners of his eyes crinkling adorably. "So, off to first period. Pretty cool we have the same English class again."

"Yeah. But you may want to think twice before starting another book report bet. I totally have a great essay idea, thanks to Hanna."

"No doubt." As his dark brows raised a few notches at her boast, he reached for her hand. They took off down the hallway until he abruptly halted. "Is this … weird?"

"Um, weird?"

Mason lifted their hands. "I mean, I'm not sure exactly how to …"

"Act?" Tessa said, finishing his sentence. They both laughed. Then, her tone turned more serious. "Actually, I know it's kinda awkward, but is it okay if we, um, talk about it every now and then? You know, so we're both on the same page."

"Like couples do," he said, squeezing her hand. "That sounds like a great idea, Tessa."

Chapter 5

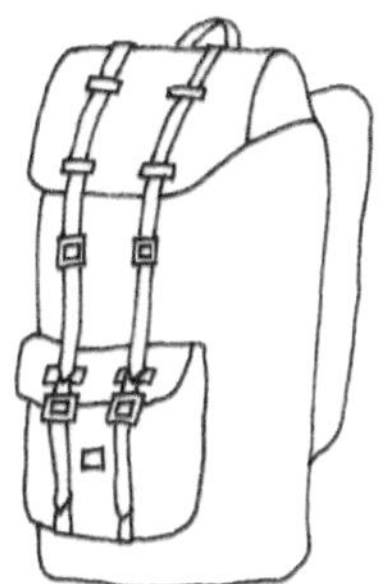

When Tessa got home from school, she was already yawning. Thank goodness Coach Powers had given them the day off from cross-country practice. But she would have to lug herself and her sports duffel to practice tomorrow. And the forecast on her phone's weather app called for a rainy day. *Another mud fest like tryouts,* she mentally groaned.

With the rain coming, she left her bike in the garage and came through the back door. She dropped her newly weighed-down backpack filled with homework onto the bench and heard rustling behind the marble island in the kitchen. "Hanna?" Tessa called out.

She was expecting to see their housekeeper's gray bun pop up with broom in hand, but instead, her dad's dark hair, slightly speckled with gray, appeared. "Hey, sweetie. No practice today, right?"

"Um, nope. Got the first day off." Taking in her dad's casual attire of a Marine Corps t-shirt and basketball shorts, she said, "No offense, but why are you home?"

Her dad laughed and went to the sink to wash his hands. "I decided to take a half-day. Do some work around the house, like this wonky garbage disposal. Hanna took Cam to see your mom at her office."

"Oh. Okay," she said, still in a tired stupor over her first day back.

She was about to grab her dead-weight of a backpack and head upstairs to do homework (before her loud brother returned) when her dad patted a stool by the island. "Come sit. I'll make you something to eat, and you can tell me about your day."

With a shrug, she flopped onto a stool, curbing another yawn. "How are things at work?" she asked.

Detective Wright passed her a bag of Ruffles, then grabbed the wheat bread and started assembling a PBJ sandwich. "Busy, as always. That convenience store was a new one, though. Nothing was even stolen."

The chip bag slipped right out of Tessa's hand. "Nothing stolen? Did someone catch the person in the act—before they had a chance?"

"Nope," he said, passing her a plate with a sandwich half. "In fact, now that the businesses have had an opportunity to review things with their insurance companies, we're finding that most have lost very little money."

Tessa chewed on her sandwich thoughtfully. "What about inventory? Are they stealing merchandise?"

Her dad shook his head. "And Murphy's Hardware seems to have lost the most cash, with that old-fashioned register." He poured two glasses of milk and joined his daughter at the counter. Tessa had to admit it was nice to spend this alone time with her dad.

"It's just weird. The whole case."

He sipped his milk. "That's for sure. So, anyway. How was school?"

"Eh, same old. Lots of homework." She tried to stifle another yawn at the thought, but this time, it surfaced. "Anyway, what about the bike connection?"

Detective Wright set down his sandwich and faced his daughter. "This was supposed to be a discussion about *your* day." When she shrugged, he sighed. "Standard mountain bike as far as we could tell. Such a bad weather day, and we were lucky to see anything before it disappeared in the rain."

You could say that again, she thought, her mind going to the not-so-blank sign that she knew was related to the bike. Unfortunately, she couldn't prove it. "Dad, who's Dan Dunbar, *Senior?*"

Detective Wright involuntarily wrinkled his nose. "He has a lot of clout, especially a town over. Whatever he's been doing, it must be going well, because he keeps expanding."

Tessa finished her sandwich. "From Westgate, right?"

He nodded, finishing his. "Yup. That's where his businesses are headquartered."

"And the delivery company is his baby, right? And really expanding around Greeneville too. I mean, the bikes are, like, everywhere."

Finishing his milk, he gave her a *Dad look.* "Tessa, what's on your mind? You've been deep in thought ever since I brought you to that break-in scene at Carmichael's."

She hesitated, wondering if he would even believe her. "When you asked me if I saw something that day, near the bike tracks …"

"And you told me you *thought* you did, then dismissed it." He set his glass on the counter and leaned close to his apprehensive daughter. "Tessa, what did you see?"

"You mean what I *thought* I saw but can't prove?"

"Can't prove?"

Tessa groaned. "You can't prove something existed when the evidence disappears. Otherwise, it's just in my imagination."

"I know my daughter. She doesn't imagine evidence. What did you see?"

Sighing, she sat up straight and looked him squarely in the same sapphire eyes. "I saw a sign."

"A sign? I didn't see any sign. Only some trash and most of it blew away." Then, his eyes brightened. "You said the evidence disappeared." He started massaging his forehead. "The rain."

"Yeah," she mumbled.

Straightening his posture, he turned back to her. "What did the sign say, Tessa?"

Taking a hard swallow of her milk, she answered, "Dunbar Deliveries. It was the same logo I saw on the ice cream bikes and the ones that do deliveries around town."

"You're telling me that it's possible the bike used in this crime *and others* was owned by Dan Dunbar?" As her dad continued to rub his temple, lines formed around his eyes.

"I'm sorry, Dad. I wanted to tell you, but I didn't want to lead you on a wild goose chase if it was nothing."

"Even though you felt like it was *something* from the start."

A sick feeling swirled in her gut. "Yeah. It's all my fault. I'm sorry."

Detective Wright sat up and took his daughter gently by the shoulders. "No, Tessa. None of this is your fault. It isn't your job to solve this. My team should have found that sign, even if it was down the block and half-destroyed." Then, he grinned as he playfully tousled her hair. "Sometimes even I forget how intelligent and intuitive you are. I should have had you comb the scene with us."

Tessa joined him in a smile. "So, I can come next time? Or help interview Dan Dunbar?"

Her dad's smile faded just like that. "No. That is not happening—ever." He started collecting the dishes and headed for the sink.

She followed. "But you just said—"

"Tessa, Dan Dunbar is a force. He has a lot of power in many circles, and you do not want to get mixed up with him."

"But I know his older son, and he's really nice."

Detective Wright stopped his cleaning and faced her with a stern expression. "Tessa, I don't trust Dan Dunbar as far as I can throw him. He has power, money, and a horrible temper. Sure, he's a successful businessman, but who knows by what means. Even an interview with him will probably prove pointless because you can't believe a word that comes out of his mouth. I'm sure even he believes his lies."

Tessa felt a shiver move up her spine. She'd seen that temper in his youngest son Troy on the basketball court and when he admitted to helping steal the State Championship trophy away from Greeneville. While Tessa had agreed to keep all of it hush-hush, content to get the trophy back in the glass case, now she was wondering if remaining quiet about Troy had been a good idea. *Especially if the apple doesn't fall far from the tree.* "So, you're saying it's dangerous. Still."

"Yes, Tessa. No question." His expression softened as he bent down and brushed hair out of her face. "This is getting longer. You letting it grow out?"

She shrugged. "Not sure yet. Maybe I'll ask Sue Ann for suggestions. She's the expert."

Their eyes held for a moment before he pulled her into a tight hug. "Thank you," he said into her ear.

"For what, Dad?"

"Being you, Tessa."

Chapter 6

Such a great day for a run," Riley said as she and Tessa walked past the parking lot where the bus let them off for their first cross-country meet.

Adjusting her new evergreen singlet, Tessa was still getting used to seeing "Cross-country" instead of "Track and Field" across the front in bright white lettering. "Great, except the location. Avondale is so snooze-worthy. Everything is so … blah-brown."

Avondale was a farming town about forty-five minutes from Greeneville Heights. It used to be bustling decades ago but had since turned into numerous boarded-up buildings on the tiny Main Street and lots and lots of brown and yellow fields. Boring, but pretty perfect for a cross-country meet.

As the team passed by the stadium labeled "Home of the Aardvarks," the two girls tried to hold back their laughter. "I still *can't* with their mascot," Riley said.

"I know. It's like they didn't even try." And their mascot wasn't the only depressing thing about Avondale. Even their dusty-brown and yellow uniforms, which blended into the scenery, were just *blah*. "I wonder if they've ever lost a teammate in the field. You know, because they were camouflaged."

Riley almost keeled over in laughter while Nick and Owen approached. "Looking good in that uniform," Owen said, nudging Tessa. "You gals gonna keep up with us today?"

She scoffed and rolled her eyes. "More like, try and keep up with us." The state had recently decided to modernize the cross-country program, so boys and girls practiced and competed together, running the same distance. Of course, awards were still given in separate categories, but Tessa loved that she would be able to outrun most of the guys on the team. She was just that fast. Pointing to the crystal-line-blue sky, she declared, "Perfect day. No rain or *mud*."

Owen nodded, clearly convinced, and ran a hand through his curly mane. There was no question he was a cutie, from muscles to his tall stature. And he'd become a great training buddy for Tessa, especially since Riley seemed to be pre-occupied making goo-goo eyes at Nick. "Well, you're easily gonna outrun Nick with his limp," Owen teased. Nick was still nursing a slight calf strain from practice and, despite his usual first-place finishes, didn't expect to pull off one today.

"It's Riley's fault for training me so hard," Nick joked, flashing her a smile.

Riley answered with her usual muteness, red face, and giggle.

But Tessa's confidence and cockiness dissipated when they followed Coach Powers down to the field and the start line for the course. She gasped. At least a couple hundred runners were scattered around the field, quite a contrast to Tessa's small track meets. "How many schools are here?"

she asked, trying to keep the shakiness in her voice to a minimum. This was *not* like track at all.

"A good portion of the state," Owen said, patting her on the back. "Pretty cool, right?"

Tessa wasn't feeling the slightest bit cool. More like sick to her stomach. She scrutinized Riley's expression and was at least grateful that she too appeared thrown. "It will be okay, right, Tessa?" she whispered. "Coach and the guys will help us."

At that moment, Coach Powers waved her team to huddle up. "Okay. I'll give everyone a chance to get acquainted with the area before we take our turn walking the course." She passed out maps and pointed to an area to relax and warm up.

Taking a seat on the grass, Tessa studied the map. She scratched her head, feeling very much out of her element. "Hey, track star," Owen said, sitting beside her. "How you holding up?"

"It's obvious, huh?"

"Yeah. You kinda look like you're gonna throw up, honestly."

Groaning, Tessa tossed the map at him. "This was such a stupid idea."

He handed it back to her. "It's not stupid, Tessa." Cocking his head at the field of runners in colorful singlets, he said, "See all of them? Yeah, you can beat most of them. Definitely all the girls—probably most of the guys."

"I appreciate the flattery, Owen, but you know I'm lost here." She looked at the map again, but it might as well have been written in a foreign language. Tessa couldn't focus on anything that intricate while panicking.

Owen lifted the map into the light. "Okay. Two miles total. Four loops is the whole course. Pretty flat for most, but there is a large hill here," he said, his index finger tracing the course map. "Remember to run on your toes up the hill. You're light on your feet, so that should be easy for you."

Tessa grimaced at the field of runners. "What about the start? It's gonna be crowded."

"Yeah. That's a bit tricky, especially since you're tiny. There can be some pushing. But they'll start us in waves, and I'll stay by your side."

She did a double take. "Really? Don't you want to go out with the fast guys?"

He shrugged. "First of all, it's a bad idea to go out too fast. It's two miles, not two hundred meters. And you're fast anyway. Plus, we're teammates. We stick together in cross-country."

Grinning, Tessa couldn't help but like Owen more and more. She was going to need the support, especially since Riley appeared as freaked out as she was.

A few minutes later, Coach Powers signaled everyone to follow her toward the start of the course. "We're gonna walk part of it and Coach will help us figure out the rest," Owen said. Tessa nodded, hoping her knocking knees would subside by the time she had to run the course for real.

Just as Owen had said, Shelly Powers, a tiny force of nature herself, led the team around the first part of the course. Occasionally, Owen would offer advice on navigating the turns. Finally, Coach Powers pointed to the hill, and Tessa's stomach dropped. The "hill" was better described as a mountain. "We have to do this four times?" She rubbed her stomach. "I don't feel so well."

Owen hooked his arm around her. "You got this, Tessa. I promise you, you're conditioned enough to do this, eight times over."

With another silent nod, she followed the team back to the start. Nick and Riley were behind them, chatting as usual. At least her bestie appeared more relaxed, even if Tessa wasn't. When they returned with the other cluster of runners, Coach Powers said, "We're in the second wave. So, relax a bit. Eat, drink, and bathrooms are behind us in the locker room, if you need them."

Tessa nibbled on a granola bar and her fingernails while the first wave took off. She cringed at the sight until her attention was drawn to a tall blonde in a Greeneville uniform. It all seemed really wrong, and her stomach clenched with discomfort. "Seriously?" she said out loud as Willow waltzed across the field *way* late. Tessa watched as she approached some girls in Avondale uniforms, her previous team (at least in track).

Owen must have followed her eyes because he rolled his. "Don't get excited. Coach isn't throwing her off the team ... yet. She got permission. I guess she moved into her new house today." Tessa had no idea how Willow had even made the team, except of course the fact that she had cut the course at tryouts.

"Not new. She's living in the old Huntington Manor."

He recoiled, using his palms as a shield. "Yikes! That place creeps me out as much as her."

Smiling, she nudged him. "So, you aren't hypnotized by Willow's charms?"

"Now, Tessa. I thought you had a better opinion of me after all those practices. You don't think I can see through all that?" Owen started jumping up and down, doing dynamic stretches.

She sighed. "Actually, you're totally my hero after owning her at tryouts. I seriously saw fear in those heavily make-upped eyes."

He was still laughing as they got last-minute instructions from Coach Powers, then lined up for the start of their wave. "Remember, don't worry about the pace on your watch. Unlike a track, each course is different. You're racing against the other runners and the terrain," Owen said.

Now, it was Tessa's turn to jump up and down, more out of anxiety than a warm-up. During their downtime, she'd jogged back and forth incessantly across the field, but nothing seemed to calm her nerves. Usually, running was what did it. "What would you say if I told you, I'm terrified?" she sheepishly admitted to Owen. Her dad once told her that when you're scared, you can either ignore it or embrace it. Ignoring didn't seem to be working today.

His eyes softened as he leaned even closer than the tight squeeze of runners required. "I'd say you're smart. Be cautious on the first loop. But I am certain, Tessa Wright, by loop three, you're gonna love it."

As Tessa waited with bated breath for the sound of the start gun, she and Riley gave each other reassuring looks. "We're ready," Riley said with way more confidence than Tessa felt.

When they heard the *blast* of the gun, it was now up to them to prove it.

Chapter 7

Like a reflex Tessa knew well, her legs took off as her spikes dug into the rugged terrain. However, she was only a few paces ahead when the elbowing and jockeying for positions increased. Owen stayed by her right side, but she soon lost Riley on her left. She spotted Nick somewhere in the mix but eventually lost him as well.

All around them was a blur of brown and green singlets, Greeneville having shared the large wave with Avondale. The sight made Tessa realize that, while the Aardvarks were only so-so in track, their cross-country team was superb. When Tessa felt a jab in her ribs from a brown singlet, she was about to give the girl a side-eye until she heard, "So sorry, Tessa," from a petite redhead.

Who the heck is that, and how does she know my name?

As Tessa shook it off, they passed the girl on their way up the daunting hill. "On your toes," Owen reminded her, and she followed his direction. To her surprise, she did feel light on her feet, although still a tad breathless as they cleared the hill to finish the first loop. Owen signaled to pick up her speed on the downhill as the crowd in the front started to thin.

By loop two, Tessa's pace was more comfortable, and she allowed herself to take in the sights around her. Despite the drab brown and yellow fields as far as she could see, the sun-drenched sky above was a stunning contrast, matching a Murphy's Hardware azure paint chip. Over her shoulder, she spotted Riley not far behind. But as they ascended the hill a second time, Nick was grimacing.

When Owen waved Tessa on to loop three, her legs were like dead weights, experiencing the effects of two trips over the hill. This time, she mentally approached the hill like a finish line on the track. *Focus on something other than the pain. Look ahead and over the hill.*

Turning the corner for loop four, Owen pulled out front slightly. She secretly wished he'd charge ahead of her and simply win this thing. But he seemed content to stay by her side. Trudging over the hill in one final attempt, Owen yelled over his shoulder, "You got this, Tessa." When she saw the end of the course in sight, her heart sang. Somehow, someway, she found something left in her to speed up.

Leave nothing in the tank, she thought—an old motto her track coach Lizzie Linden would say.

With muscles screaming, Tessa finished her first cross-country race at the front of the pack, just behind Owen. As she collapsed to her knees, her legs spent and numb, he patted her on the back. "I told you, track star. You loved it, right?"

Still gasping for breath, she wanted to slug him (and his *rainbows-and-butterflies* disposition) but didn't have enough energy to lift her arm. Tessa wouldn't say she "loved it," but, no question, she was thrilled to receive her place card for the race. Now, she had to be patient and wait for the rest of the waves to finish to see where they placed overall.

Both Riley's and Nick's faces did *not* convey that they loved the course as they led the way for more evergreen and brown singlets to follow. When Nick crawled over the finish with a pained expression while grabbing his calf, Coach Burgess and Coach Powers rushed to his side. Tessa and Riley shared a worried look.

Then, Tessa's gaze was drawn back to the course as the last of the runners jockeyed for final positions. She immediately spotted the red-headed girl in the brown Avondale singlet who apologized earlier and knew her name. Unfortunately, it was the girl coming up on her rear who stole Tessa's focus—Willow. She clearly was trying to pass the Avondale girl but didn't seem to have much left in her. Tessa thought her eyes were deceiving her when Willow elbowed the petite redhead so hard, she stumbled and nearly fell to the ground. *She's your old teammate,* Tessa mentally scolded Willow.

"Tessa!" she heard and was shocked to see her mom and Mason waving from several yards away.

She ran into her mom's arms with a burst of energy she didn't know she had left and then hugged Mason. "What are you guys doing here?"

Dr. Wright raised her eyebrows at Mason. "I'll let him explain while I go and congratulate Riley."

"So?" Tessa asked when her mom had disappeared.

He flashed her a coy grin. "When you told me about your meet, I called your parents to see if they were going. And here we are. Your dad got called into work at the last minute, unfortunately. Awesome finish, by the way, keeping up with Owen."

Baffled, Tessa stumbled over her words. "Wait. Um. You know Ow—"

"Hey, man. Long time," she heard behind her as Owen stepped up. He slapped Mason's hand while Tessa looked on, confused.

"Mason and I go way back to basketball camp as kids," Owen said, handing Tessa a bottle of water from a nearby cooler.

Mason laughed. "Yeah. That's when I thought you'd be playing with me someday, not running."

"Eh. Gotta do what you're good at. Although, you guys are a little sluggish on the court, *Captain.*"

"No, you're right. That's why we train with the likes of the amazing track team." Mason affectionately wrapped his arm around Tessa's shoulders.

"Well, your girlfriend can run. That's for sure." Owen downed some water, then said to Tessa, "I'll go check on our overall placements and see if there's an update on Nick." He bumped fists with Mason before rushing off.

This whole dialogue intrigued Tessa. It made sense that two really nice guys would be friends, but how did she have no idea? Then, she realized she hadn't said anything to Mason about training with Owen. After a complicated series of interactions with Nick during the summer, she figured it was better to speak in more general terms about her practices. But clearly, Owen was aware that she and Mason were an item.

"I didn't know you two were … friends," she said to Mason.

"Oh, yeah. Owen's a good guy. Great shooter too, if he ever decides to stop running. Which, based upon that finish, he shouldn't."

Tessa kicked around some patches of loose brown grass with her shoes. "Sorry I didn't mention training with him."

Mason squeezed her shoulder. "Tessa, it's fine. I shouldn't have acted the way I did about Nick that time."

"So, I guess we both messed up a little."

A sweet smile formed on his lips. "Yeah. A little. It's no biggie."

"You're also a good guy, Mason Greene."

As they walked back toward the finish chute, he said, "Your mom was trying to explain this sport to me. How is the scoring done again?"

Tessa chuckled. "Let's find Owen and he can explain. I have serious runner's brain after trudging up that hill four times. You're lucky I remember my name."

As Tessa glanced back at the course and that steep hill underneath a picturesque deep blue sky, she had to admit that she was starting to love it. Maybe not as much as track. But it was growing on her, for sure.

A couple of hours later, Tessa and Riley were snapping dozens of selfies, hoping their creative poses jazzed up the yawn-inducing blah background. Tessa modeled two golds (one for her own placement for the eighth-grade girls and one for the team), and Riley proudly displayed her team medal, having placed an impressive Top Five. "Not bad for our first race," Riley said, elbowing Tessa as they walked back to the parking lot.

Just then, a bike whizzed by with its rider shouting, "Ice cream! Refreshing ice cream!"

"Is that an ice cream bike? In Avondale?" Tessa asked.

Riley squinted into the distance. "Looks like it. The sign says Dun—"

"Dunbar Deliveries." *Just. Great.*

Chapter 8

"The party starts in less than an hour, Tessa. Do we have time?" Riley asked outside of *Once Upon a Bookshop* in downtown Greeneville Heights.

Tessa cupped her hands around her eyes and peeked through the front windows. "They really do such a great job with the displays here." She pointed to several cute montages utilizing a variety of titles from classics to modern best sellers.

Riley hugged a wrapped gift to her chest, anxiously darting her gaze down the block. "It will take us ten minutes to walk to the bowling alley. Don't you want to be early to see Mason before everyone else?"

Pulling herself from the windows' allure, Tessa rolled her eyes. "You just want to see Nick."

"Well, it was nice of Mason to invite him to his birthday party."

"Yeah. Mason is a nice guy. Anyway, we won't be too long. Just a quick sleuthing exercise. I have a hunch."

Riley reluctantly pulled open the door under the green awning imprinted with the outline of an opened book. "Fine. Let's get this over with."

Immediately, they were greeted with a refreshing *blast* of cool air. Tessa breathed in deeply, enjoying the aroma of rich coffee beans mixed with freshly printed pages. "I love the smell of books," she said, running her fingers over a hardcover propped up in a front display.

Riley gave another eye roll, trying to get to the point of their visit. "So, what time was the break-in?"

"My dad said Friday evening or Saturday morning. That's why he couldn't make it to our meet. Dorian was frantic. Apparently, this place was a disaster afterward."

The girls skimmed the quaint bookshop, meticulously organized by genre and age-group. The children's section was nestled in the back with an inviting reading area of tiny chairs and floor cushions. Tessa had fond memories of this place from her childhood. Her mom would practically drag her back outside. But she always left with a crisp, new book.

A small coffee bar was positioned along the opposite wall from the main register area. Usually, the whole place would be crammed on a late Saturday afternoon, with children's book readings and parents enjoying frothy, caffeine-laden beverages in comfy leather armchairs. But currently, the shop was deserted. "This isn't good," Tessa whispered.

"I know. It's creepy being here alone, especially after the break-in. Maybe we should just go."

Riley was about to spin toward the door, when the owner (eccentric Dorian McClellan) appeared out of nowhere, making her jump. "May I help you, ladies? Oh, Tessa, good to see you again," he said, recognition setting in.

"You too, Dorian. How are you?"

He pushed his dark, thick-rimmed glasses up his nose with his index finger. "It's been better. At least the store is back in shape. Took me hours over the past week."

"Sorry to hear that. Has it been slow all week?" she asked in a sympathetic tone.

Dorian's face looked pained. "It's not easy keeping a brick-and-mortar bookshop open as it is these days. But Greeneville has always been such a great place to have a business. Not so much anymore, I guess."

Tessa's heart sank. "Are you considering closing or relocating?"

"I'm keeping my options open. Most of us business owners are getting calls inquiring about selling. Everyone is on pins and needles right now." Dorian carefully adjusted some books on a nearby shelf, pushing them back into perfect alignment. "Is there anything I can help you find?"

Tessa didn't even have to think twice. "Well, I realized I'm missing the next book in my *Nancy Drew* series. It's the fifth one."

Dorian's eyes brightened as he waved them down the narrow yet tidy aisles. "You have got to be kidding me," Riley murmured.

They passed the register area, and Tessa paused a moment to admire the extensive bookmark section, including one in dark leather. "Mason would like this," she said. Getting Riley's stink eye, Tessa hurriedly caught up with Dorian.

"*The Secret of Shadow Ranch,*" he said, holding up the book to the light. "Such a great ghost story. Spooky enough for upcoming Halloween." He started to hand Tessa the small hardcover with Nancy riding a horse on front, then hesitated. "But it is the newer version. I kind of prefer the original 1931 edition. Ah, to be able to have an antique book section."

While Dorian continued to stare off into his own world of hopes and dreams, Riley let out an exasperated sigh. Tessa relented and took the book. "Yeah. This is perfect. I'll take it."

Relieved to make a sale, Dorian gleefully ushered them over to the register. "We just got those copies in too. New delivery right before the break-in, so I'm glad they didn't get damaged in the mess."

As Tessa pulled her wallet from her crossbody purse, she perked up. "Oh. Did you, um, lose a lot in the break-in?"

"No, thank goodness. I always keep the register empty when I leave at closing. So, it was basically only a mess, including the coffee area." He involuntarily shivered, placing his hand over his heart. "Imagine the horror if they'd gotten coffee or pastries on any of the books!"

Riley tapped her foot repeatedly on the carpet, eyeing her watch. "Definite horror. For sure." Tessa shot her a jab with her elbow.

Handing over some cash, Tessa explored further. "You said a new delivery. Was it a big one?"

Dorian focused on lining up the bills perfectly in the register before counting out Tessa's change. "Oh. We're small here and so are all our deliveries. I'd rather keep tabs on what sells and order when necessary than keep a stock of unpopular items."

"So, you use bike deliveries, then?"

Lifting his chin, he nodded as he handed Tessa a few bills. "Yes. Such a great thing for the environment, isn't it? And Dunbar delivers right from the post office or the shipping companies. No dirty delivery vans to clutter up gorgeous Main Street."

Even Riley's attention was now piqued. "Um, we'll take this too," she said, reaching for a leather bookmark embossed with small basketballs. "And could you wrap it?"

Without uttering a word, Tessa handed Dorian more cash. "I'll be right back. What type of wrapping? The occasion?" he asked.

As Tessa stared, dumbfounded, Riley volunteered, "Oh, a birthday. Tessa's boyfriend."

When he'd left, Tessa turned to her best friend with narrowed eyes. "What the heck was that? I thought you wanted to get out of here ASAP. The guy is a perfectionist. It might take him an hour to wrap that bookmark."

"Tessa, as it is, we're going to be late. I don't know much about guys, but my parents did push the manners. You gave Mason his gifts early, but we can't exactly show up with that bookshop bag and not have something for him."

Her face reddening, Tessa now realized her shortsightedness. "Sorry, Riley. Sometimes, I get a little too much into …"

"The sleuthing. I know, Tessa. And I actually think you were right coming here."

"Really?"

Riley nodded, then silently pointed to a flyer sitting behind the register. She covertly peeked over her shoulder, then quickly plucked it, handing it to Tessa. "Here. Read and I'll keep a lookout."

"You're brilliant, Riley." Tessa swiftly skimmed the flyer, brimming with information from Dunbar Deliveries. It was obviously focused on businesses in Greeneville Heights' Main Street and pushed special "introductory rates." When Tessa's gaze moved to the bottom of the page, she noticed a line of towns encircling her own and starting with Westgate. "I think these show their expansion. Avondale is on here."

"And like a dozen others. Geez, they're surrounding us."

"Or squeezing us," Tessa said. "Wait. This says this is the 'Shipping Division.'"

Riley wrinkled her nose. "There are others? I thought it was just a delivery business."

"Nah. My dad said Dan Dunbar is pushing hard to expand. Let's see what else he does." Tessa used the flyer as a reference and typed his website address into her cell phone.

When the opening page flashed a massive photo of Dan Senior himself, Riley cringed. "Geez. Talk about an ego. His photo covers most of the home page."

Tessa laughed. "I know, right? He's like the perfect textbook villain," she said, pointing around the bookshop.

Joining her in a giggle, Riley continued to swipe from page to page. "What the heck? Dunbar Enterprises? He is … everywhere. Even real estate. It's like the guy wants to take over every town for miles."

As Riley's fingers scrolled her phone for several minutes, Tessa found herself shuddering instead of laughing. Dan Dunbar's stretch seemed infinite. "Something feels really creepy about all this," Tessa said. "I'm certain he's involved in everything happening around downtown."

Riley was suddenly quiet, just like the eerily deserted shop. "Yeah, Tessa. I think your hunch was right."

Chapter 9

When Tessa and Riley raced out of the bookshop with the most beautifully wrapped package on the planet, they had only three minutes to make the ten-minute-long journey. Riley was right; they were going to be late to Mason's party. But when they passed an ornamental streetlamp with a large flyer advertising "Dunbar Deliveries," Tessa had to check it out.

"This one is asking for drivers . . . probably because they've expanded so much," she said. Scanning the flyer, she let out a whistle. "No wonder they can acquire such a huge staff. See that incredible hourly rate? They really must be doing well financially." Then, lifting it off the post, she scoffed. "Seriously? They put this one up over another delivery company's flyer—Davies Deliveries. That's pretty inconsiderate." *Talk about flattening the competition.*

"Ooh, the Amateur Astronomy Society!" Riley shouted, grabbing the deep blue flyer below dotted with twinkling stars. "I've always wanted to join this. And it says they're planning a huge event at the park this fall, for the upcoming meteor shower."

"That does seem cool," Tessa said, reading the details. Then, she started chuckling. "Oh, my gosh! We're the worst with distractions!"

Riley's eyes magnified through her glasses as she pocketed the flyer. "I know! The party!"

Exactly seven and a half minutes later, the two track stars skidded to a halt at the entrance of Greeneville Lanes. Riley bent over at the waist, then attempted to fuss with her long, dark hair. With a roll of her eyes, Tessa pulled her through the glass door. "Come on. Nick is waiting."

Stepping inside the local bowling alley was like revisiting the past. With the exception of impressive disco lighting installed for the "Rock 'n' Bowl" nights, the place never seemed to change. For the evening's festivities, the music was at ear-shattering levels, which, combined with the frequent *crash* of balls against pins, made conversation a challenge. "I'm gonna find Mason," Tessa shouted to Riley. As they veered off in opposite directions, Tessa didn't even have to ask who her best friend was looking for.

Passing by the shoe rental counter, Tessa decided to save some time and grabbed her usual size six and headed to the busy lanes of teenagers.

Mason was easy to spot, in the center of well-wishers, many of whom were impressively tall. It was clear he had invited the entire basketball team. But it was a fifty-fifty split of boys to girls. While there were faces that Tessa couldn't place, most were good friends or acquaintances at their tight-knit middle school. As she hurried to join the group, she admired the mouth-watering spread of food, from pizza to wings and even cheesy nachos. She was eager to taste test the steaming, gooey mozzarella sticks when it occurred to her where the loud music was coming from. Along the far wall, Mason's brother Alex (at the helm of the drums) and his band were finishing belting out a set. It really was a fantastic party.

Tessa was relieved when Mason's eyes locked with hers and he rushed to greet her. She was hoping to chat in private before the chaos reigned. "Hey! You made it!" he said, hugging her tightly.

Without missing a beat, she said, "I'm so sorry Riley and I are late. It's my fault."

Mason appeared slightly taken aback, then checked his watch. "Oh. I wasn't keeping track of the time. Is everything okay?"

"Yeah. I had this … hunch and needed to get some quick sleuthing in. But unfortunately, it wasn't as quick as I'd hoped. Oh, and this is for you—peace offering." She passed him the long box wrapped in dark blue paper scattered with glittery stars, similar to the astronomy flyer. A silver iridescent ribbon was delicately tied around it. Tessa figured the wrapping must have cost Dorian way more than he got from the sale of the actual bookmark.

"Wow. You're getting even better with this wrapping stuff. Is that double-sided tape?"

"Yeah. Like my mom uses. But I didn't wrap it. Got it at the bookshop."

Mason nodded appreciatively but with a perplexed expression. "You already gave me gifts, though. You didn't have to do this."

Tessa gnawed on the inside of her cheek. She really was horrible at this girlfriend stuff. "I just wanted to … apologize. I shouldn't have put sleuthing ahead of … well, you."

As another deafening *crash* of pins made them flinch, he slung his arm around her, guiding them to a quiet corner.

"Tessa, you don't have to apologize. It's just a party. And you're here, so that's what matters."

Her face flushing a warm, deep pink, she gestured to the box. "Open it."

After carefully removing the ribbon and placing it in his pocket, Mason ripped open the paper with one sweep of his fingers. "See? I'm learning," he teased. When he lifted the bookmark from the box, he beamed. "This is so cool. I could use one of these."

"And, happy birthday, again," she said, pulling him into another hug.

"Come on. You're on my team. We're totally gonna kick Caleb's butt." As they walked up to the rowdy lanes, he whispered into her ear, "So, your hunch. It was right, wasn't it?"

"Yeah. It was."

They approached the crowded lanes, and through the chaos, Caleb screamed, "The girlfriend is here!"

Instantly, Skylar shot him a swift punch in the arm and grabbed Leah. "We're on Mason and Tessa's team," she shouted back to her brother.

He gave her a fake look of betrayal, but it wasn't entirely phony because Skylar happened to be the best bowler in the group. Losing her was a royally stupid move. "Whatever," he grumbled. "Leah's still on my team."

Leah's gaze bounced back and forth between the twins, clearly torn. "You can play with Caleb if you really want," Tessa said, nudging an eye-rolling Skylar. "No hard feelings."

Just then, Riley and Nick joined them. While Nick sported a calf sleeve, Tessa was pleased to see that he no longer walked with a limp. After a few days off from practice, he was moving around much better. "I'm so ready to bowl," he said, rubbing his palms together.

"We're just picking teams," Mason said.

"Well, pick already, birthday boy," they heard through the music. Tessa turned and her jaw dropped to the floor, seeing Owen's curly hair and bright smile through the dazzling disco lights. With a fist bump to Mason and a wink at Tessa, he took a seat to slip on his shoes. Mason hadn't said that he was inviting Owen, but it made sense considering they went way back.

"Who's the hottie?" Skylar whispered to Tessa, with Leah lifting her strawberry-blonde brows in agreement.

"So … teams," Mason started.

"I have an idea," Owen said, getting everyone's attention. "How about guys against girls?"

Skylar crossed her arms and scoffed, "You sure you wanna do that?"

"Yeah, Owen. Sky bowls like 200," Tessa said, enjoying the fact that she could brag about one of her best friends.

Owen lifted his own eyebrows but didn't seem deterred. "A team's more than one person, right, Mason?"

Appearing torn himself, Mason turned to Tessa, who shrugged. "Sounds fine to me." *After all, I'll have Skylar!*

"Okay, then," the birthday boy declared. "Let's bowl."

Chapter 10

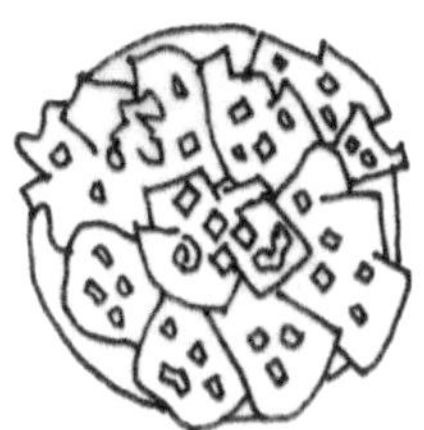

Skylar was poised at the end of the lane, her gaze tight and laser-focused ahead as her hands gripped the glittery purple ball. "You got this, Sky!" Tessa shouted, on the edge of her rigid plastic seat.

Then, Ethan appeared through the front door. His arm was adorned with both a wrapped gift ... and Willow. With the band taking a break, a *hush* fell over the room and Skylar turned to see what all the commotion was about. As the pulsating techno music resumed overhead, she shook it off with a huff and a determined gaze back to the pins. Starting her approach, she wound back and hurled the ball with such force it slammed against the shiny wood floor. *Bang* and *roll*. Everyone held their collective breath as the purple ball crashed into the headpin. It ricocheted around the pin deck and knocked down one pin after another until no pin remained standing.

"Yesss! We win!" Tessa cheered, grabbing the girls in one team embrace.

Skylar sauntered back to her team with her head held high. "That would be a strike, boys," she said, smirking. "*Another* one."

Mason applauded and gave Tessa a wink while Caleb sulked. Meanwhile, Owen extended his hand to a blushing Skylar. "Impressively bowled, Ms. Abernathy."

"I think someone is crushing on a new guy," Leah whispered to Tessa. "At least he isn't a jerk like—"

Ethan approached Mason after lagging in the shadows. "Happy birthday, man." Willow was no longer by his side, choosing to forgo the pleasantries and linger by the front door.

"Oh. Thanks," Mason said, looking a bit like a deer in headlights. Ever since Ethan and Skylar's falling out, the guys had decided to tread lightly, mostly restricting their relationship to just teammates. But Tessa could tell that Mason was too nice of a guy to exclude Ethan from his party. She had a suspicion that he hadn't expected Ethan to actually show *and* with Willow.

"Let's get some mozzarella sticks," Skylar said, grabbing the girls. "I saw them drop off a fresh tray."

The girls were downing stringy cheesy goodness when something caught Tessa's attention out of the corner of her eye. A built guy, who appeared more imposing than she wanted to admit, entered the back room of the bowling alley carrying a bike helmet. Tessa went rigid when she noticed the vest he wore said "Dunbar Deliveries." "Um, I'll be right back," she told her friends.

"Come back soon. I think I see the nachos on their way." Skylar dipped the end of her cheese stick in spicy marinara while Tessa headed for the opposite end of the room.

Despite the recent crime wave and anxieties around town, Greeneville Lanes was still bustling on a Saturday night. One area had been reserved for Mason's party, while another was sectioned off for the competitive leagues, leaving a few lanes for the general public. As far as Tessa could see, every square inch of the building was filled. It was a relief to see one business doing especially well.

With people occupying every corner, it was difficult for Tessa to weave around the crowd and make it to the back. But when she did, she found the delivery guy had completed his drop-off of boxes and was waiting for a signature from the manager. But the manager didn't seem so keen on any of this. "What are you doing here? I called Davies to do this."

Big Burly Guy simply shrugged. "I just go where I'm told. You'll have to take it up with your boss."

Davies? As in, Davies Deliveries? The names were similar. Was it possible that someone got things mixed up? Tessa didn't know Greeneville Lanes' owner very well, but he was an elderly man. Sweet, but getting up in his years. She could see how he might have made a mistake. Whatever it was, the manager didn't seem happy about it. And the delivery guy appeared as though he was trying his patience with every wave of his finger.

"You can tell *your* boss that I'm not paying this delivery fee. You guys used to be the cheapest. Your prices have gone up three-fold just this summer."

Big Burly Guy's face was getting redder by the second, and Tessa was worried he might explode. But instead, he turned his back and slid on his helmet with a "Whatever. You Greeneville lot are all the same." He stormed off in a heavy-footed huff, leaving a chill that ran up Tessa's spine.

Pretty rude guy. And definitely odd.

"Everything okay?" Mason asked, pulling her from her thoughts.

"I should ask you that." She pointed at Ethan, who was chatting with Caleb. Willow was nowhere to be seen.

Sighing, he ran his fingers through his dark waves. "Yeah. Sorry about that. I didn't think he'd—"

"It's okay, Mason. It's your party. And Skylar is tough."

"You're right about that." She gave his cryptic answer a blank stare. "Oh, just ask her."

When Tessa returned to the snack table, her friends were scarfing down a piping-hot tray of nachos, the cheesy mountain piled high with a topper of lettuce and pico. "What did I miss?"

Leah dropped her chip and leaned in. "You missed Sky freaking Willow out so much that she totally bolted."

"How?"

Skylar was enjoying a gooey bite, so Riley interjected, "She started talking about how spooky her new house is. Willow clearly had no idea of that place's history."

Tessa's eyes grew wide. Huntington Manor was the creepiest house imaginable. The stories were notorious, although no one was sure they were even true.

Finally finishing her nacho, Skylar waved everyone close. "Hey. Instead of our usual meeting, what do you say we do some sleuthing?"

Intrigued, Tessa perked up at the very notion. "What do you have in mind?"

"A haunting."

Chapter 11

"It's not *that* bad, right?" Riley whispered to her besties, hunched over several tall, misshapen boxwood hedges.

Tessa cocked her head, scrutinizing the dilapidated Victorian home in front of them. She couldn't help but cringe. While it may have been lovely and even impressive in its prime, it currently exuded more Freddy Krueger than *Architectural Digest*.

Leah involuntarily shivered. "I swear this place was the backdrop for some horror films."

"What the heck are we doing here, Sky?" Tessa asked, stretching out her sore back with a sigh. She loved a good stakeout as much as anyone, but so far, all they'd learned in the past half hour was that Willow's parents had hired the laziest moving company in town.

"Pizza in the treehouse sounds way more fun than picking ants off me," Leah groaned, smacking at her exposed ankles. In lieu of the girls' usual Sunday afternoon meeting, Skylar had suggested they conduct a stakeout of

Huntington Manor. But she had yet to explain why or what she hoped to achieve.

"Come on. Let's go," Riley said timidly, pulling at Skylar's tank top.

"Wait!" Skylar said, swatting her away. She silently pointed to the front of the house, where tall, blonde, and annoyingly perfect Willow sauntered out the door and onto the spacious porch. A visibly exasperated Ethan followed as Skylar nodded. "Exactly."

Tessa squinted at the scene and whispered, "Uh, what *exactly* are we supposed to be seeing here?"

Ethan audibly groaned as Willow pointed to a huge box labeled with her name. He rolled his eyes before picking it up and bringing it inside, and Skylar chuckled. "I've seen that look before. He's totally over her, *finally*."

Standing up straight, Tessa put her hands on her hips. "Are you serious right now? We're here because of Ethan?"

Skylar shook her head. "No, that's bonus entertainment." When all three girls gave her the same *you've-got-two-seconds-to-explain* look, she turned and pointed to the house.

Ethan stuck his head back outside with the same box and yelled to Willow, "What room again?"

"I told you! Second floor. First one on the right! With the round window!" Huffing, she flipped her blonde locks behind her shoulders before opting to grab a floor pillow in lieu of a box labeled "Willow's Books."

"Scary, right?" Skylar said, facing her friends.

Tessa nodded. "Yeah. Who would have thought Willow actually owned books?"

Skylar let out a long sigh. "No. Willow is using *that* bedroom. You know, the most haunted room in the whole house." A collective *gasp* could be heard from behind the hedges.

Huntington Manor was notorious in Greeneville Heights. Of course, every town had its own haunted house. Tessa figured most of the stories about this particular one survived for lack of anything else better to do in their quaint town. Up until the recent string of break-ins, life in Greeneville was comfortably predictable.

"Isn't that the room where that girl lived? The *wanderer* or something?" Leah asked, deep in thought.

Skylar's eyes got as big as silver dollars. "Yeah. According to the legend, she used to live here, in that room, then disappeared by nefarious means. But her ghost is still seen wandering by that round window." Then, she waved her hands around dramatically, creating mystique. *"Her red hair framed by the delicate arch of the window."*

"Oh, good grief!" Tessa groaned, face-palming. "Can we go now?"

Out of the blue, Riley's phone vibrated, making everyone jump. "Sorry, guys." One glance at the text message and she blew out some frustrated air. "My mom wants me home. Now." Riley's parents were driven surgeons at Greeneville Heights General Hospital, so they always had tight schedules. But they'd become even more stringent with Riley's ever since they'd decided to split up.

"I'll go with you. I gotta watch Missy anyway, or she's bound to get into trouble," Leah said, referring to her younger sister.

As the four girls left their positions behind the hedges, Skylar stole one more glance at the house. Ethan had returned, massaging his lower back while Willow rushed him down the porch steps. "Come on," Tessa said, pulling her friend away.

A few minutes later, Tessa and Skylar were heading home with Creamsicle pops from one of the Dunbar Deliveries ice cream bikes. "They really are everywhere, aren't they?" Skylar said, licking her pop.

Tessa gave the bike an apprehensive glance. "Yeah. They really are. But ice cream season is pretty much over."

"I guess they'll have to come up with another business to keep them busy."

Truer words, Tessa thought. "So, anyway. What was up with that fake stakeout?"

"It wasn't fake. We got … information." Tessa flashed her an *I-wasn't-born-yesterday* look, and Skylar relented. "Fine. At Mason's party, Willow was going on and on about her great house and Ethan helping her move in."

"And you wanted to see if any of it was true."

Skylar lifted her shoulders in a shrug as she licked her ice cream pop. "Maybe."

"Sky, I thought you were over Ethan. You remember how he broke your heart—twice?"

Skylar paused their walk and faced Tessa. "Of course, I remember. But I also remember good things too. I mean, he didn't act totally happy back there, right?"

Tessa's eyes bulged as she nearly dropped her ice cream. "Have you been talking with him again?"

Staring down at her feet, she murmured, "A little. At the party." When she looked up to Tessa's narrowed gaze, she said, "And last week when he came over to play basketball with Caleb."

Tessa tried to hold her patience, but her loyalty to her friends was unwavering. Ethan had hurt Skylar in the deepest way possible. It wasn't something she could easily forget or forgive. But she knew, in the end, it wasn't her choice to make. "Just be careful, okay, Sky? Don't be a Willow."

Skylar grimaced and downed the rest of her ice cream pop. "No one wants to be a Willow. But I wouldn't mind if she got a little haunted now and then."

As the girls headed down the quiet blocks of Greeneville Heights, they linked arms and laughed the whole way home.

Chapter 12

"Go forth and do great things!" Mr. Stuart cheered as the bell rang, ending another long week. He always concluded his eighth-grade Honors English class paraphrasing Ralph Waldo Emerson, but Tessa never ceased to be inspired.

"Are we on for this bet, *officially*?" Mason asked, zipping up his backpack. He was referring to the essay on their summer reading, due in only a week.

Tessa adjusted the evergreen and white spirit corsage (a reminder of tomorrow's meet) on her cross-country t-shirt, fanning herself with her notebook. Fall had yet to arrive in Greeneville Heights, and Tessa had no idea when she would be able to pull out her favorite track jacket. "Of course, we're on, Mason Greene. I'm almost done with my first draft, and I can guarantee you'll be treating me to a Lorraine Combo sooner than you think." She could practically taste the hamburger, curly fries, and milkshake at their favorite 1950s diner.

"And onion rings. Don't forget about those," he said as they walked out of English class, laughing at their light-hearted bet.

"Oh, I would never. That's the best part." Heading down the hall, Tessa took Mason's hand. He seemed to smile even brighter.

"You excited for your meet? Sorry I can't come." As captain of the basketball team, his coach was sending him off on a weekend sports leadership camp.

Tessa shrugged it off. "No biggie. My parents are both working, so they can't make it either. And River Valley is a couple of hours away."

When they reached Tessa's next class, Mason lingered a bit. "I still wish I could come, but I'm sure you'll do great."

"I don't know. River Valley is full of fast girls"—including Tessa's major track rival Carly Mahoney. "And Avondale will be competing too."

"Well, I have no doubt you'll be adding another medal or two to your collection." Mason glanced up at the hallway's digital clock and reluctantly released Tessa's hand. "Have a good class. See you at lunch." He dashed into a nearby classroom just in time for the bell, leaving Tessa grinning all the way to her seat.

A few hours later, Tessa was working on squats in the weight room during cross-country practice. Owen waltzed in and perched himself on one of the machines. "Looking good, track star."

"Thanks," she said breathlessly, grabbing a couple of free weights. "How's Nick doing? I saw Coach Burgess talking with him. Good news?"

Owen paused his workout to sip his water bottle. "Yeah. He's cleared for tomorrow. I guess his calf is back to one hundred percent."

"So, you have some competition now." She flashed him a smirk, knowing the two guys were friendly rivals. Up until Nick's injury, Owen had never beaten him in a race.

He laughed, appreciating her teasing. "We'll see. After training with you, I'm even faster. Nick has his work cut out for him."

They were chatting through their workouts when a picture-perfect Willow sauntered in. Tessa had to turn away just to hide her enormous eye roll. How on earth was her hair photo-shoot-ready even during cross-country practice? Then, again, it was clear Willow wasn't one for hard work.

Through the reflection in the wall of full-length mirrors, Tessa caught Willow flipping her hair back gracefully and leaning over Owen's machine. "Hey, cutie. You think you could give Tessa and me a minute to talk?" she purred with her sweetest smile.

He stopped his latest rep and shot Tessa a look that silently asked if this was *okay*. She nodded, and he headed for the door without a word. Before Owen disappeared, he turned and mouthed a "good luck" to Tessa, forcing her to suppress a chuckle.

"What's up?" she asked Willow, continuing her bicep curls.

Willow sighed like having this conversation was painful. Tessa couldn't disagree. "What does your agency charge?"

Tessa did a double take, the 10-pound dumbbells nearly slipping out of her hands. "What did you say?"

"What. Does. Your. Agency. Charge?" Willow enunciated each word as though Tessa was incapable of understanding English.

"My detective agency?" Tessa wanted to add, "Why do you care?" because since when did Willow care about her at all, let alone her agency? Instead, "Why do you ask?" escaped her mouth.

Crossing her arms and thinning her gaze, Willow said, "Because I may be interested in your services."

Now, Tessa was intrigued. She bit her lip to keep from smiling. "Actually, we don't charge. We don't do it for the money but to help people. And if those people are especially grateful, sometimes they give us donations."

None of this seemed even vaguely interesting to Willow. In fact, Tessa was positive that once she'd finished the first sentence, Willow had tuned her out. "Anyway. I'm interested."

"What's the issue?"

Willow hesitated and peeked over her shoulder. "What experience do you have with, um, ghosts?" It was spoken barely above a whisper.

Grabbing a mat from a stack behind her, Tessa had to stifle some laughter. *If only Skylar were here to witness this.* "Well, I don't personally know any, but I'm open to introductions. With friendly ones, that is."

Willow did not seem amused by Tessa's sarcasm. "What are you doing?" she asked as Tessa lowered herself to her floor mat.

"Planks. You know, practice. You should try it sometime."

Winding her blonde hair between her fingers, Willow rolled her eyes. It was obvious this was the most effort she was putting in for the day. "Oh, whatever, *track star*. Are you going to help me or not?"

Tessa let several beats of thoughtful silence go by while she finished her plank. She couldn't resist. It was too fun making Willow squirm. "Depends. What exactly do you have in mind?"

"I don't know. Do you do seances? Remove spirits or something?"

Sitting up from her plank, Tessa wrinkled her nose. "Do you even know what a detective agency does?"

"Well, no."

"Clearly. It certainly isn't seances. We investigate. I take it this has something to do with your new house."

Instead of her usual confident sassiness, Willow appeared uncomfortable. "Yes. But my parents don't believe me. So, will your agency help me or not?"

Everything was telling Tessa to say 'no,' including Skylar's voice in her head. But the curious side of Tessa-the-super-sleuth was seeping through. "I can't promise anything. I have to see what the rest of my agency says. We're a team." Something she knew Willow cared nothing about.

Willow turned slightly pale. "You mean … Skylar."

"Yup. She's part of the team."

"Fine. Whatever. Let me know." She stomped out of the weight room and almost ran smack-dab into Owen, who made a point of dodging her like the plague.

"Wow, Tessa. What the heck did you do to push her off her throne?" Owen asked while Tessa resumed her planks.

"Don't ask," she said, catching her breath. "I'd rather do a hundred planks. That says it all."

Owen was still laughing as he returned to the weight machines. But Tessa's mind wasn't on her planks at all.

Chapter 13

It was another gorgeous day for a cross-country meet. As Tessa adjusted the bib on her singlet, her best friend retied her shoelaces. Standing up vertical, Riley grimaced. "That bus ride really was brutal. I think my butt is still numb." Laughing, Tessa had to agree. It was over two hours long, navigating bumpy, rural terrain around several bodies of water. But at least she'd managed to finish her new *Nancy Drew* book. "How on earth did you read through all that?"

"Many years of practice, my friend," she said, moving on to help Riley with her own bib. "River Valley is pretty, though."

"Oh, by the way, Carly was looking for you. Wanted to say 'hi' before her wave." Despite being track rivals and fierce competitors for their teams, Carly and Tessa were always cordial, respectful, and the epitome of *sportswomanship*.

When Riley jetted off to meet up with Nick, Tessa followed the cluster of orange and black singlets indicating the River Valley Cheetahs. "Tessa Wright!" Carly shouted, craning her neck to spot her tiny competitor. "I can't believe you finally joined the ranks of cross-country. What took you so long?"

The girls gave each other quick hugs. "Eh. Peer pressure?" she joked. "I'm still getting my trail legs, so take it easy on me."

Carly laughed. "Whatever. I know you won last weekend. It's fun keeping up with the guys though, right?" Then, she lowered her voice, jerking her neck toward Nick and Owen in the distance. "And, you have some attractive ones."

"Yeah. They're good guys."

Carly stood back and regarded her. "So, it is true." Tessa responded with a blank stare. "You're seeing that seriously cute basketball guy."

Tessa could hardly believe her ears. Even River Valley knew she was dating Mason Greene? "Um, yeah. I didn't realize it had gotten around."

"Eh, small sports world."

All of a sudden, Tessa's gaze was drawn to a head of blazing red hair wearing a brown singlet. "Hey. Who's that girl running for Avondale?"

"Oh. That's Amelia Davies. She's really good and light on her feet. Just gets pushed around by the bigger runners."

Tessa's mind conjured up an image of pushy Willow. "Yeah. I noticed that at our last meet." Motioning toward the redhead, Tessa said, "Amelia knew my name."

"Tessa, everyone knows your name. You're a state champion."

"Oh." Tessa tried to rub off the blush blooming on her cheeks. "So, good luck today."

Carly slapped Tessa on the back as her team headed to the start. "You too and watch the second turn. The view is great, but the trail is crazy uneven."

"Thanks for the tip, Carly."

Later, when her own team was lining up at the start, Tessa still had the previous meet on her mind. "You ready to win this one?" Owen asked, nudging her playfully. "I'm certainly not gonna with Nick back in the game." He pointed behind where Nick was wearing a serious expression. As he shut his eyes, his torso would tilt back and forth while running the course through his mind.

"Carly says turn two is a bit uneven," Tessa said absentmindedly.

Owen's usual cocky smile faded. "You okay?"

She crooked her finger at him to move closer, then nodded at Amelia in front of them. "You think you could, I don't know, block anyone from pushing her around?"

He gave her an incredulous stare. "You mean, you want me to protect your competitor?"

Tessa sighed. "Willow elbowed her pretty hard at our last meet. It wasn't right."

Owen considered her request for a long moment until his lips upturned. "You got it, track star."

When the gun went off for Tessa's wave, she was positive Carly would win hers. Even though both Tessa and her rival were more experienced on the track, their running talents and competitiveness seeped through on any surface.

As the mammoth cluster of runners converged down the first embankment, Tessa kept her eyes on Amelia. Then, she cracked a smile, watching Owen succeed in blocking and protecting the tiny Avondale runner from the worst of the elbowing and shoving. Without getting nudged so severely, she pushed out front easily.

Tessa, on the other hand, found herself getting knocked about. Being several inches shorter than most of the guys, she had to duck to avoid an elbow here and there to her ribs and even her head. But she wasn't afraid to push back.

She deserved a space in this wave as much as everyone else. Eventually, the clump of runners spread out, and Tessa was able to charge ahead on the heels of Amelia and several of the faster guys, including Nick (who clearly looked intent on winning the race).

When they reached the second turn in their first loop around the rugged course, Tessa paid particular attention. True to Carly's warning, while the water view was lovely, the trail was quite rutted. As Tessa noticed several runners get lost in the beauty around them, then nearly wipe out, she had a sinking suspicion someone truly would before the day was done.

Making it safely around the turn, Tessa allowed herself to glance up at the cloudless sky. With low humidity and a refreshing breeze off the water, the day had that crisp on-the-cusp-of-autumn feeling. The trees were still green, but occasionally, you'd spot a dot of color among the foliage. She found herself enjoying the area and her run, especially once she'd established a rhythm.

Through the second, then third loop, Tessa was holding her place behind (leader) Amelia. Starting the final loop, Tessa got a second wind and shot forward with a burst of energy down the embankment, almost flying past Amelia.

As they approached the tricky terrain, Tessa was nearly even with the redhead and shouted, "Watch out!" steps before Amelia landed on a scary crater of earth. The petite Avondale runner swerved just in time, then accelerated as though she'd found her own second wind. With a kick that Tessa guessed rivaled only her own on the track, Amelia sprinted to the finish.

Meanwhile, Tessa was so preoccupied with Amelia's progress and avoiding the trail's uneven spots, she barely skirted the water's edge—and ran right into a massive swarm of gnats. Despite swatting them away, instead of a gulp of fresh autumn air to aid in her final push, she sucked in several tiny insects and managed to choke and cough her way to the finish.

Tessa crossed to cheers from Nick and Owen (who had obviously finished first and second), as well as from Coach Powers. "Nice, strong finish, Tessa."

But Tessa didn't need her own place card to know that she had finished second. Owen gave her a look that only the two of them shared. If he hadn't protected Amelia as she had requested, Tessa would have won. She shrugged at Owen and mouthed, "It's okay."

She then approached Amelia (who remained hunched over, catching her breath inches from the finish line) and patted her on the back. "Great race, Amelia."

The petite redhead glanced up with astonishment in her light eyes. "What? Really?" Amelia clearly couldn't believe she'd won, let alone against the likes of Tessa Wright.

Seconds later, Riley appeared in the cluster of finishers, smiling brightly. Tessa and her teammates cheered as she passed through the finish chute. "Congrats," Tessa said to her best friend.

"What place did you get?" Riley asked Tessa instantly.

"Second in this wave." Riley's agape mouth proved she was shocked. "But Nick won. Check out that smug look all over his face directed at Owen." They both laughed at the guys, throwing water bottles at each other instead of doing their cool-down like Coach Burgess kept shouting.

Tessa was still recovering from the insufferable gnats when Owen passed her a water bottle and examined her carefully. Wrinkling his nose, he attempted to curb his laughter while pulling something off her hair. "What the heck happened to you? Was this part of your master plan to help Amelia?"

She groaned and shook her head vigorously. "No. Absolutely not. I got too close to the water and … the bugs."

"Yeah. That's another thing about cross-country, track star. It's buggy."

Of course, it is. "Thanks for the advance warning," she said sarcastically, inspecting strands of her hair for any stragglers. "I must have inhaled several dozen."

"Hey, it's protein, right?"

As he continued to laugh, she smacked him with the water before downing the entire bottle.

The rest of the meet was a whirlwind, with top team finishes as follows: 1st place to Greeneville, 2nd place to River Valley, 3rd place to Avondale. Amelia won first overall, followed by Tessa, and then Carly. Tessa knew that if Amelia hadn't been in her wave, pushing her so strongly to the finish, her time might not have beaten Carly's. So, secretly, they had done each other a favor. Nick had fun razzing Owen by shoving his gold medal in his face.

And, even though Tessa loaded the bus with only one gold medal, she appreciated the silver even more, watching Amelia stare at her own gold in disbelief, surrounded by her thrilled teammates.

"I think you made Amelia Davies' week," Owen whispered.

"Well, she deserved to win with that kick."

And then a thought came to her. *Davies?* Why did that name sound so familiar?

Chapter 14

"Any other old business?" Tessa asked during the girls' usual Sunday agency meeting, waving her gavel in the air of the treehouse. When she received a silent response of headshaking, she took a steadying breath. "So, new business, then."

"Yeah. Do we have any new cases? Things have been slow lately, just like downtown," Skylar said, nibbling on a granola bar.

"Dead is more like it," Leah chimed in. "I went to Murphy's Hardware yesterday for some paintbrushes, and Chuck was eating his lunch at the register. Like, full-on *sandwich-on-the-counter-picnic-spread.* He said I was the only person he'd seen all day."

Tessa's eyes grew bright. "Even on a Saturday?" But this wasn't really a surprise. *The break-ins.*

Riley lifted her head from her secretary's notebook. "I think people are bypassing Greeneville and going elsewhere."

Leah sifted through the snack bin, finding a new bag of Doritos. "Yeah. Like Westgate. They just built a nice new hardware store there. Even Chuck sounded interested in checking out his competition."

"This isn't good," Tessa said, her mind temporarily sidetracked from her original worry.

"Anyway, so new business. What new case do you have for us, Prez?" Skylar asked.

Circling her table, Tessa leaned against it. She knew this next vote would be a contentious one. "Well, it could be interesting. Not our typical lost bike or cat. Kinda spooky. Perfect for this time of year."

"Stop stalling, Tessa. What is it?" Leah groaned, pulling her orange fingers from the depths of the Doritos bag.

"Fine. It's investigating Huntington Manor … for Willow."

Silence enveloped the treehouse as the girls gave Skylar apprehensive glances. Tessa practically cringed as Skylar opened her mouth. "Sounds fine to me. You got my vote, er, second," she said with a shrug, then returned to her granola bar.

Tessa's gavel slid right out of her fingers and landed on the treehouse floor with a *thud*. "I'm sorry. What?"

"Yeah, Sky. You don't have a problem with helping Willow?" Riley asked, pushing her glasses up from the tip of her nose.

"Nope. It's about time she groveled and asked for our help." Then, she turned to Tessa, looking giddy. "She totally begged you, right?"

Picking up her gavel, Tessa shrugged. "Kinda. I mean, she was certainly worried that I was going to say 'no,' especially after we brought it to a vote."

"Good," Skylar said, beaming.

"What exactly are we supposed to investigate?" Leah asked. "We're not gonna find anything. Even if it's a ghost, it's not like they leave evidence."

"It might not be a matter of *what* but *why*," Tessa said, rounding her table and moving the gavel from one hand to the other.

"Why?" Riley repeated.

"Yeah," Tessa said, leaning forward across the table. "All those in favor of solving *why* Huntington Manor is being haunted." When four hands shot through the air, Tessa slammed her gavel hard on the table. "Hold on to your hats, ladies. We've got a ghost to find."

Chapter 15

Later that day, Tessa hummed a pleasant tune while strolling through downtown Greeneville Heights. Main Street was lovely any time of the year, but autumn gave off its own cozy aura. Spotting baskets of colorful puffy mums, plump pumpkins, and hay bales lining the sidewalks was a comforting sight. She conjured up an image of families, hand in hand with little kids in their coolest superhero and princess costumes, stopping by local businesses for candy. Tessa could already taste the caramel apples and creamy hot cocoa that Lorraine's served on cool nights. But seeing the empty streets, even on a Sunday, was disappointing.

When she passed a vacant storefront, she halted, unable to believe her eyes. Anna's Florist Shop, where Tessa and Mason got each other's corsage and boutonniere for the spring dance, had disappeared like it was never there. Tessa's stomach sank. Anna had done a wonderful job with the peonies Tessa had requested. Then, she noticed the front window. Instead of floral displays of beautiful arrangements collected into breathtaking bouquets, a large sign blanketed the space with "For Rent" and then "by Dunbar Realty."

Tessa steamed as she passed more buildings, some with advertisements for "Dunbar Deliveries" or for "Dunbar Enterprises." Now, on the verge of tears, she turned and peered down the vacant street of what used to be bustling downtown Greeneville Heights—no longer predictable and maybe on the verge of "no longer" completely.

She was still trying to calm her erratic heart rate when she turned the block near the new police complex. But seeing her dad wasn't a planned stop for the day. The toll of a church bell down the block snapped Tessa into action, and her eyes flicked to the nearby clock tower over City Hall. Shooting a quick wave toward the modern police building, she rushed to the old brick library.

A pair of columns flanked the entryway as she climbed the marble steps and entered the tall vestibule. This place was usually a respite for Tessa; even the smell of the old books was comforting. But today, she couldn't see past the devastation of her walk.

Due to the late hour, instead of browsing, she hurried straight for the curved circulation desk, where an older woman with half-rimmed glasses stood. She was carefully examining the condition of several hardcovers in a tall stack. "Tessa!" she said in the kind of whispered excitement that only a seasoned librarian could accomplish.

"Hello, Linda," Tessa said, relaxing against the desk.

The two knew each other well—maybe too well. "You doing all right, dear?" she asked, clearly noticing Tessa's diminished mood.

She shrugged. "It's okay. I'm hoping you'll make it better."

"Of course. I found the copy right away. What do you think?"

Tessa had called ahead of time. After finishing her latest *Nancy Drew: The Secret of Shadow Ranch*, she couldn't wait to get her hands on a copy of the original 1931 version. In lieu of Nancy poised atop a horse, this hardcover book was a simpler solid blue with a silhouette of the main character. "Wow. I can't believe you have this. The bookshop didn't."

"Well, we do have a nice antique book collection that we borrow out from time to time. And we happened to have a couple copies of this gem."

"It's supposed to be really different from the other version, which was only so-so." Tessa handed Linda her laminated library card, which she scanned. "I'll take good care of it."

"Oh, I have no doubt, my dear. Anything else I can help you find?"

Tessa's gaze swept the large space, then landed on a small table near one of the back windows, with a view of the shaded courtyard. "I'm gonna browse for a little bit."

"Of course. And you're all set with this." She carefully handed the old book to Tessa, who in turn cradled it in her arms.

Heading straight for the table, Tessa noticed this space was also an example of the crumbling downtown, with not another soul in sight. She tried to shake it off as she approached the girl wearing a brown "Avondale Aardvarks" t-shirt. Her red head was bowed, fully engrossed in a hardcover of *Little Women*. "Hey, Amelia."

The girl sat up in shock. "Tessa Wright," she murmured in disbelief, like she was staring at a celebrity who somehow managed to infiltrate the library on an ordinary Sunday afternoon.

"That's a good one," Tessa said, pointing to Amelia's book. "Which one do you think you are?"

Still stunned, Amelia answered, "Um, what?"

"Which sister? I think I'm more of a Jo, but then again, maybe my friend Skylar is. She also plays the piano like Beth. And my friend Leah is artistic like Amy, but totally not stuck-up. I guess we're all a mix."

As Tessa outlined the finer points of her English essay, Amelia stared open-mouthed, then whispered, "Um, I guess I'm kinda like Beth. Definitely socially awkward and shy."

Tessa took a seat across from her. "We're all socially awkward." This made Amelia smile. "And my best friend Riley is shy. But she opens up with her close friends."

"Riley is on track and cross-country with you, right?"

"That's right." Tessa's phone vibrated in her pocket, but she ignored it.

"Everyone on Greeneville's team is so friendly. Well, except for …" Then, she bit her lip. There was no question who the "except for" was referencing.

"It's okay. You're talking about Willow, right?"

Nodding, Amelia fidgeted with the straps on her backpack as her petite frame appeared to shrink behind it.

"But Willow used to be your teammate." *Buzz. Buzz. Buzz.* Tessa once again ignored her phone.

"You can get that if you want."

"Nah. That's okay." Then, something occurred to her. "Hey. What are you doing so far from Avondale?"

Amelia slipped her book inside her backpack, and Tessa couldn't help but smile, seeing the gold medal sticking out of it. "My parents are divorced. My mom lives in Avondale, but it's my dad's weekend and he lives here." Then, she rolled her eyes. "Of course, he has to work, but still wanted me to come. Sounds crazy, I know."

"Actually, one of my friends is going through that too with her parents."

Another smile lifted the corners of Amelia's lips. "It's tough, but everyone on the cross-country team has been so nice. Speaking of being nice, I wanted to thank you."

"Thank me?" Tessa croaked as her throat went bone-dry.

"Yeah. You warned me about that turn. Otherwise, I wouldn't have won."

Relief washed over Tessa. "Oh. No biggie. You were faster, so you deserved to win." Her phone vibrated again, and she let out a *groan*. "Sorry. Let me get this." But as she read the text messages, she started beaming from the inside out. "It's my ... *boyfriend*." Tessa was still having trouble getting used to the word.

"Is that the cute Owen guy on your team?"

Tessa shook her head vigorously. "Oh. No. Owen's just a friend. It's, um, Mason Greene. He was away all weekend. I guess they didn't let them use their phones, so he wanted to know how the meet went."

"He sounds really sweet." Then, Amelia's own phone buzzed in her backpack. "Mine is from my dad. He's picking me up."

As the girls walked out of the building together, Tessa offered her a slip of paper. "Here's my cell number. If you're ever in town when your dad has to work, give me a call. We could hang out."

"Wow. That's so nice of you, Tessa." When a truck pulled up, she slung her backpack over her shoulder and headed down the steps. "Oh, and I'd steer clear of Willow. She's a bully."

Tessa nodded, knowing what she said was true. But there clearly was more to the story than meek Amelia wanted to divulge.

But, as she jumped into the white truck, Tessa noticed the sign along its side and her mind went into overdrive.

That's where I've seen that name before. Davies Deliveries. A direct competitor to Dunbar.

Chapter 16

Despite her upbeat conversation with Amelia, Tessa was in a royally awful mood when she stepped over her front door's threshold, clutching her vintage *Nancy Drew* novel. Another walk back through her beloved Greeneville Heights, currently a ghost town, was enough to make her blood boil, especially spotting several more signs highlighting the word "Dunbar."

As Tessa started for the hallway leading into the kitchen, she heard cooing and knew her mom was interacting with her baby brother. She certainly didn't have the patience for that nonsense. Doing an about-face toward her bedroom, she heard, "Tessa, sweetie?"

With a grimace, Tessa turned back. "Hey, Mom," she said, hesitantly entering the living room where a blanket was spread out. Cam was positioned on some spongy chair, doing a rare thing in lieu of screaming—giggling.

Tessa paused several yards away as her mom sat up on the blanket. "He's cutting a tooth, so this is probably as happy as he'll be for a while," she joked.

No kidding, Tessa thought. She produced a simple nod and started for the hallway again.

"Sweetie," her mom called after her. "You okay?"

Trying to suppress an exasperated sigh, she spun back around. "Yeah. I just want to read in peace." Her eyes darted from Cam and back, and her mom got the drift.

"I filled up your snack chest in the treehouse if that works better than upstairs. I can't guarantee peace for longer than ten minutes at a time."

"Thanks, Mom."

When Tessa reached the backyard's sparkling lap pool, she considered dipping her feet in. Refreshing summer swims would soon be a thing of the past, replaced with autumn chill and fallen leaves, scattered and skimming the water. But the weight of the antique book between her fingers jogged her memory, and Tessa bypassed the pool and headed for the treehouse.

Armed with a crisp and juicy McIntosh apple—fall's best gift—Tessa sank into her beanbag chair and dived into another sleuthing adventure with her favorite heroine. But, only five pages in, she couldn't even recall what she'd just read. Her mind was elsewhere—like deserted downtown Greeneville. Groaning at the ceiling, she stared at the empty bulletin board, usually filled with cases for the agency. *Empty—just like Main Street.* Maybe she could fix both.

Grabbing a spool of red string from Leah's art bin, Tessa started tacking up sheets of paper and connecting them with the string. She'd used this *link analysis* in a previous case, and it had given her some clarity. But it also had the tendency to make things even more complicated.

Her outer ring was the downtown businesses and owners hit by the *string* of break-ins. There were so many that Tessa got chills seeing the large circle, even while cozy warm inside the treehouse. Only one owner, her hairstylist Sue Ann, was injured by the perpetrator, and Tessa couldn't help but think it was a fluke. She had been the only business owner there after-hours.

Time for some deductive reasoning. What do I know that is true? A bike was used in one of the crimes—a Dunbar Deliveries bike. Tessa was sure of it. But no other witnesses or evidence of a perpetrator existed. And her dad had emphasized that no sign of breaking in *actually* occurred in any of the locations. *An inside job?* Very little money and no merchandise was taken. *Could it be like the haunting of Huntington Manor? It isn't who but why that matters?*

She tilted her head back and rubbed her eyes. "What is going on?" she moaned. "It's like I'm chasing a ghost or fake crimes." But they seemed very real to the town. Enough to spook everyone out of downtown. Then again, maybe that was the point.

"Tessa! Mason's here!" she heard her mom's voice call, and she jumped. This was a surprise. Tessa wasn't expecting to see him so soon after his leadership weekend.

"Just a second!" she yelled, not sure what she could possibly do in that small fraction of time to look presentable. Pushing her unruly hair back with her headband, Tessa really was regretting not seeing Sue Ann. Her jeans and track t-shirt weren't her most impressive look but would have to do in a pinch. After a quick glance at the selfie mode on her cell phone's camera, she gave up and headed for the ladder.

Mason was relaxing on the patio, petting a snoozing Watson while Sherlock bolted off to the side yard to chase a bird or get into some other kind of trouble. As Tessa approached, she noticed Mason's evergreen sweatshirt and squealed inside. "Hey. Sorry to keep you waiting. Nice surprise."

Lifting his chin from Watson, he beamed at her. "Well, I missed you, so ..."

They met each other in the middle of the yard, both acting shy. Tessa was the first to reach up for an embrace. "Um, how was your weekend?" Mason was all warm cotton, a comfort she was easily getting used to.

"Good. Lots of team building. Can't wait until practice starts soon." His green eyes sparkled in the late afternoon light. "What about your weekend? Congrats on the meet."

"Thanks. It was pretty fun. Well, that part of the weekend anyway." Tessa shrugged, waving him to the treehouse. "You wanna come up?"

Mason gave her a coy nod. He was still hesitant mounting the ladder to the formerly *Girls Only* treehouse. When they'd ascended the maple's limbs, he asked, "What do you mean? The rest of your weekend wasn't fun?"

Sighing, Tessa offered him a soda, then pointed to her bulletin board. "It's been more like this mess."

"So, you're back at it with the string, huh? Didn't the finished look seem more serial killer than *CSI?*" They both laughed.

"It kind of is. But remember how last time I had too many suspects in the trophy case? Like everyone could have done it?"

"Yeah. And they practically did. It was a conspiracy, like you suspected."

Tessa pointed to the blank space in the middle of the large circle. "Now, it's like I have *no* suspects. As in, *no* crimes, either."

Mason took a sip of his soda. "Wait. You're saying the break-ins aren't real crimes? They sure seem real. My mom said business is down on Main Street like seventy-five percent." Lauren Greene was the mayor of Greeneville Heights and had been working overtime, just like Tessa's dad, to calm and reassure the community.

Tessa expelled some frustrated air. "I don't know. I mean, I think Dan Dunbar is involved. But I don't even know if I can prove it. That evidence disappeared too."

"Dan Dunbar? You mean the guy who owns the delivery company or his son Danny? And what evidence disappeared?"

Setting down her soda, Tessa took a seat at the table and detailed her experience at the Carmichael's crime scene and what she was sure she had seen but couldn't prove. Then, she explained Dan Dunbar's company expansion. Pulling out her cell phone, she found the already-opened tab with Dunbar's massive website.

"Yikes. Creepy headshot," Mason said, scrunching up his nose. "Makes him look guilty or even like a book villain."

Suddenly, Tessa went rigid as a connection zapped through her brain like a jolt of electricity—the bookshop. Riley's words: *"He is . . . everywhere. Even real estate. It's like the guy wants to take over every town for miles."*

Then, there were all those businesses closing downtown, including Anna's. Even Dorian was considering relocating his bookshop. *When he got calls inquiring about selling.* And the signs were plastered all over town. "Dunbar Real Estate," Tessa whispered.

"Huh?" Mason asked.

Tessa ignored him and scrolled frantically through her phone as tingles ran up her spine. When she clicked on the "Real Estate Division," her heart was pounding so loudly, it rivaled Alex Greene's contributions to his rock band. "This says he buys up depreciated properties. As in, he takes businesses that have lost value off people's hands."

Mason sat beside her with wide eyes. "Tessa, you're right. No way that isn't related to our dying downtown."

"That Dunbar is buying up bit by bit."

"Wait. But you said your dad interviewed Dan. What did he find out?"

Tessa shook her head. "My dad said it was as useless as he suspected. Dan lawyered up. He was cordial, but it was clear he wasn't going to let anyone stop his expansion."

"I wish I knew if my dad was involved in the questioning." Mason's dad was the town's top prosecutor. "But he keeps that stuff confidential, even from his son."

Mason rolled his eyes and Tessa chuckled. Then, a light bulb clicked over her head. "*His son*, Danny. Do you think it's possible he has some information?"

"I don't know, Tessa. Unlike his brother Troy, Danny is a good guy. Don't you think he'd tell the police if he suspected something?"

Tessa tapped her chin. "Maybe. But not if he doesn't even realize he knows something. It might be right in front of his eyes."

"Okay, super sleuth. When are we interviewing Danny?"

Giving him an incredulous stare, Tessa said, "Wait. You wanna come with me?"

Mason dug out his leather wallet from his jeans and pulled out the tiny button that Tessa had given him over the summer. "I'm an official member of the agency, right? It's my job."

"You carry it with you?" Tessa thought it was a sweet gesture. Then, she noticed a photo tucked away in a plastic protector. The vibrant floral backdrop indicated it was the professional one of the pair, taken at the spring dance. Tessa wore a turquoise dress with a peony corsage adorning her wrist. She had a copy of the same image but kept it in a frame on her nightstand.

When Mason noticed her eyeing the photo, his cheeks turned an adorable scarlet. "It's a nice photo of us."

"My hair was a bit less wild," Tessa said, adjusting her headband.

Mason leaned over and touched a few strands of her hair. "Oh. I figured you were growing it out. It's nice either way."

"Thanks." Now, it was Tessa's turn to blush. "You're pretty great, Mason Greene."

As they locked eyes, Tessa once again wondered if he was going to kiss her—*really* kiss her. Butterflies swirled in her stomach in anticipation. Staring into his remarkable eyes, Tessa felt his warm breath tickle her neck before his lips touched her cheek. When he slowly pulled away, she couldn't say she was disappointed. Just surprised.

"So, we're in this together again, huh?" he asked softly.

"Absolutely."

Chapter 17

"*The Outsiders* was pretty good, but nothing is gonna top my *Little Women* essay. I can already taste the ranch dripping from the onion rings," Tessa boasted to Mason on their way to her locker after school. Earlier that day, they'd turned in their summer reading assignments and couldn't stop teasing each other about their "colossal bet."

Mason relaxed his shoulder against the bank of lockers as Tessa spun her combination. "Oh, I agree your idea was good. And I do see a lot of Jo in you. In all the characters. Except Amy. Never liked her." He made a grimace while Tessa giggled.

"Well, I see some Laurie in you."

He grimaced again. "But he ends up with Amy."

"Yeah. That was another idea I had for an essay. *Why Jo should have chosen Laurie, despite Alcott's resistance.*"

Enthralled, Mason leaned in close. "What was your top reason?"

"Easy. They were the best of friends."

He beamed. "So, what exactly is the plan tomorrow for your cross-country meet at Westgate?"

Cupping her hand around her lips, Tessa whispered, "I was thinking we could stop by the delivery company. Apparently, Danny works on Saturday afternoons, so it will be perfect—"

"*Ahem*" carried across the space, interrupting Tessa. She whirled around to find Willow's scowl and crossed arms while holding a stack of envelopes.

Knitting his dark brows, Mason whispered to Tessa, "Should I be worried?"

"Nah. She's harmless. Sort of. I'll fill you in later." He nodded and gave her a quick kiss on the cheek.

"See ya, Mason," Willow said in her fakest attempt at politeness as he passed by with a wave.

"What's up, Willow?" Tessa asked, slamming her locker.

"You two are as sweet as maple syrup. It's pretty nauseating."

Tessa tried to hold back an eye roll. At least Willow had stopped with the faux niceties. Those were nauseating too. "I take it this is about the case."

"Yes. I recorded some video like you asked." Willow pulled out her cell phone and played a few seconds of a poorly lit room and a window.

Tessa lifted the phone and squinted at the screen, then shook her head to herself. "What exactly am I supposed to get from this?"

Willow let out an exasperated sigh. "Can't you see the curtains?"

"Yeah."

"They're *moving!*"

"Willow, you had the window open. This doesn't prove anything other than the fact it was breezy last night."

With a huff, Willow ripped her phone out of Tessa's hand and replaced it with a pumpkin-orange envelope. "Fine. Here."

"What is this?"

"It's an invitation to a Halloween party. At my house. I thought you could come and investigate. And, with a party as cover, the whole house would be available without giving my parents a clue."

Tessa ripped open the envelope. "That's actually a good idea."

"I know," Willow said, looking very pleased with herself.

Inside the envelope was a paper cut-out of a haunted house, ironically, with a party invite for Halloween night and a request to wear a costume. "This is a really nice invitation. I'm used to the evite ones."

"Yeah. I also have digital ones for the guests farther away. But my mom's a second-grade teacher and was way too excited to make these."

Tessa slipped the invitation into her bag. "Oh. My mom's a—"

"A doctor. I know." She rolled her eyes, clearly not impressed. "We had to see her a couple of weeks ago when my two-year-old brother got strep. She's the least annoying pediatrician we've seen since he came out of the womb."

"Uh, thanks?" Bonding with Willow was clearly going to be difficult, if not impossible. "I didn't know you had a younger brother."

"Yeah. He's been screaming ever since he was born. Thankfully, he won't be at the party." A screaming brother was something Tessa could relate to, even if Willow wasn't.

"Anyway, can you give these out to everyone else?"

"Uh, sure," Tessa barely got out before Willow thrust more envelopes at her and jetted off down the hallway.

When Tessa sifted through the stack of envelopes, she noticed they were addressed to all of her friends (and fellow agency members), including Willow's archenemy, Skylar. Mason and Caleb were also in the mix. Tessa had no doubt that Willow had rushed off to deliver ones to Nick and Owen personally before cross-country practice. Overall, it didn't seem like a bad way to spend Halloween or such an awful case after all.

"Now, all I need is the right costume for a night of sleuthing." As she dropped the envelopes into her backpack, she found the perfect thing to give her some inspiration.

Chapter 18

"It was nice of her to invite us, even if it has to do with the case," Riley said to Tessa, depositing the orange envelope into her duffel bag. Heading to the start of their next meet, they crossed a flat, nondescript field surrounding Westgate's main concrete block building. "But I doubt I'll go anyway."

Tessa did a double take, stopping to retie the laces on her running shoes. "Why not? It's Halloween!"

"You know I'm not a party person, Tessa." Riley fiddled with her bib for the umpteenth time. "Even if my parents will let me go, which would take a lot of coaxing."

Pulling her friend over to the closest half-alive tree on the school campus, Tessa whispered, "Don't you see what a great opportunity this is?"

"Uh, no."

"This is your chance to ask Nick out on a date."

Riley's jaw dropped to the sparse, brown grass-covered ground. "But … isn't it too soon? I mean, shouldn't we wait a little while longer?"

"You're stalling, Riley."

"But I don't even know what to say, Tessa."

With a sigh, she deadpanned, "I think 'would you like to go to the party with me?' about covers it."

"But what about costumes? Do we each pick our own or do a couple's thing, even though we're not a couple?"

Riley was still droning on and on when Coach Powers signaled the team to walk the course. However, after a short stroll, it was apparent that this course was in no way scenic. In fact, it appeared to be the most boring and depressing run of the season—very fitting for the rest of Westgate.

"Did you see that obnoxious billboard visible from the first turn?" Riley asked.

Tessa certainly did, nodding her annoyance. "I can't believe they let Dan Dunbar advertise like that, yards from the school. It's a giant replica of his egotistical website."

Just then, Owen and Nick came up from behind. "Is everyone ready for the most unexciting run of their lives?" Owen joked.

"I know. The whole course is just flat dirt. Even Avondale has grass. Why do they even host meets here?" Tessa asked.

Riley appeared to have lost her voice as Nick chimed in. "Hey. Compared to other courses, this is easy. And Avondale and River Valley aren't here, so we should win, no problem."

Tessa had to agree, especially after their previous difficult meet. But, even with a bug-free course, the last thing she was looking forward to was five loops around the same brown scenery with a mega-sized view of Dan Dunbar's head on the first turn. "That billboard reminds me of the creepy eyes in *The Great Gatsby*," Tessa whispered to Riley, who giggled.

The meet was as uneventful as they feared and as successful as they hoped. Greeneville won the team competition and swept the individual medals, with Tessa placing first and Riley second. Nick and Owen were once again one and two, respectfully, although it was an exciting sprint to the finish. But that was the extent of any excitement for the day. To top it all off, Tessa didn't even enjoy her run and found herself cringing at the start of each loop, wishing she could hide from the prying eyes of Dan Dunbar.

Mason was the brightest part of the day (well over her two gold medals) when she saw his adorable grin at the finish. Tessa told her parents it was fine to miss the meet, especially since she had some top-secret sleuthing scheduled for the rest of the day.

Tessa was about to ask Riley to come along when she spotted her bestie cornering Nick as he performed his intricate cool-down routine. *Just ask him, Riley!* she mentally nudged.

"So, Alex can pick us up after his band practice. Are you ready?" Mason asked, his eyes twinkling with eagerness.

This snapped Tessa back into business mode. "Um, yeah. You texted Danny that we were stopping by, right?"

"Yup. He said he'll tell the front desk, whatever that means."

It means we're venturing into their territory—Dan Dunbar territory.

The short walk to Dunbar Enterprises would take them along Westgate's dead downtown area. Once a booming industrial town during the turn of the century, when the factories closed decades later, most residents left, taking their businesses with them. Tessa remembered skirting the area that summer on their way to a pick-up basketball game at the school. So, this time, she wasn't expecting much in the realm of attractiveness for their Main Street, especially considering the bland, rundown appearance of most of the town. But the moment they entered the downtown area, Tessa noticed stark differences from the last time she was there.

New sidewalks had been installed with lovely vintage streetlamps, reminiscent of downtown Greeneville Heights. In fact, a lot of the changes were very Greeneville-esque. Fresh, colorful flowerpots dangled from the lampposts. Even the road had been paved with bright paint outlining the numerous crosswalks. If Tessa were searching for green grass, this was where she would find it—in tiny park areas with leafy trees, encircled by fragrant mulch. She was certain this was the only place in Westgate with living trees and grass, but no one walking their dogs or running with strollers seemed to mind.

But the influx of new businesses really got Tessa steaming. Restaurants were aplenty with patrons filling the outdoor seating areas. Tessa swore she saw a Greeneville resident or two in the mix but tried not to let herself watch too intently. She and Mason remained painfully quiet as they passed a lovely bookstore with a welcoming awning and signs advertising an "antique section." And of course, Tessa's heart sank seeing a sign for a new florist shop. She hoped it wasn't Anna's, but she couldn't fault her. There were more people milling about than she'd seen for weeks in Greeneville. But, to top things off, everywhere they went, Dan Dunbar's face or his company's logo greeted them. From real estate, to restaurants, to financing, and ultimately, his delivery "division"—Dunbar Enterprises had its hand in every shiny new flowerpot.

"You okay?" Mason asked. Sensing her mood, he wrapped his arm around her. "You'll figure it out, Tessa. You always do."

"I don't know, Mason. This is a lot bigger than a missing skateboard or trophy. My dad says this guy is really powerful and not to be trusted."

And if they were questioning exactly how powerful Dan Dunbar was, they needn't look any further than the behemoth of a glass building in the distance. Tessa halted, feeling like Dorothy staring at the gigantic glowing Emerald City. *We're not in Greeneville anymore, Mason.*

"Together," Mason said, taking her hand and squeezing it.

Tessa swallowed hard and stepped forward. "Together."

Chapter 19

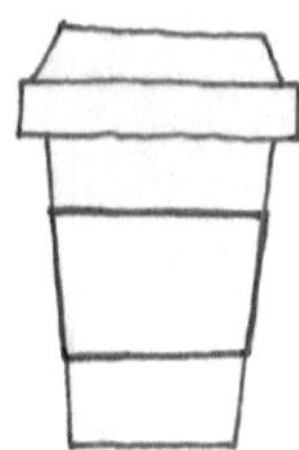

When Tessa pushed through the revolving door of the modern office building with Mason on her heels and holding her cross-country duffel, she was glad she'd already changed from her singlet and running shorts. But even her cross-country t-shirt and jeans didn't seem appropriate enough for the fancy lobby with the large circular desk of dark granite. "That must be the *front desk*," she whispered to Mason.

"Looks like it."

The two approached the desk with caution and waited for an older woman to look up from her, also fancy, laptop. "May I help you?" she asked with very little enthusiasm and no eye contact.

"Um, yes. My name is—"

"Tessa Wright!" she heard from the back doorway as Danny Dunbar removed his bike helmet and approached. "And Mason Greene," he said cheerfully as he shook both their hands. Then, he turned to the rude receptionist. "I got this, Nina."

"Thanks for meeting with us," Tessa said, relieved to dodge the tight security of the grumpy front desk.

Danny waved them past Nina's perpetual scowl and over to a small coffee bar near the expansive, open lobby. "No problem. I just got back from a delivery run in Greeneville, so this was perfect timing." He approached the barista and motioned his hand across the massive menu overhead. "What will you have? It's on me, or rather, my dad."

Tessa mulled over the menu with a blank stare. "Um, just a coffee, I guess." She could count on one hand the number of times she'd had coffee in the past and it was usually only for the caffeine rush.

"You sure? Our pumpkin spice lattes are all the craze this time of year."

"Sure. That's fine," she said. Mason agreed and Danny ordered.

When they found a quiet table near a window facing a heavily shaded courtyard, Danny eyed them over his frothy latte. "What do I owe this surprise? Last time I saw you guys, you were riding off into the sunset with that trophy. Rightfully so, I might add. And thanks for keeping it between us."

Tessa sipped her latte, grateful it contained heaps of sugar. "Of course. It was all a bad prank, and the trophy is back where it belongs."

"Well, it was stupid of my brother and his friends. But you're right. Water under the bridge, I guess. So, what's up?"

Before they could answer, another guy wearing a bike helmet and a "Dunbar Deliveries" vest appeared. Tessa thought he looked vaguely familiar. "Hey, Danny," he grumbled.

"Your dad wants me to do the rest of the Greeneville runs today. You got the list?"

Furrowing his eyebrows, Danny dug into his pocket. "Really? He didn't tell me that. Here," he said, giving him the list. "Call me if you have any problems."

The guy let out another grumble and walked away while Danny rolled his eyes. "Sorry about that. Rex is only on the payroll because my dad knows his stepdad from the zoning board. But the guy's a nightmare."

"Rex?" Mason asked, clearly noticing some recognition as well.

"Yeah. Rex—"

"Jamison," Tessa finished.

Danny stopped his coffee mug halfway to his mouth. "You know him?"

"I ran into him in the park one day." *More like ran AFTER him . . . stealing Rocky Redmond's amazing skateboard.* Mason's eyes bulged at her as he nodded his agreement.

"Sorry to hear that. He's like the worst employee ever. We've had a few like that, but as long as they can do heavy lifting, my dad doesn't care." Tessa couldn't help but remember the burly delivery guy at the bowling alley. He definitely wasn't big into customer service, but she was sure he could lift a hundred pounds, easy.

The longer Tessa sat there, pretending to enjoy her latte, the more apprehensive she was becoming about being in Dan Dunbar's building. Something seemed really off. "We passed several Dunbar billboards and signs on the way here. You guys are really expanding."

"Yeah. My dad wasn't happy owning one small company. I guess he wanted an empire." Danny shrugged, finishing his coffee. "Honestly, I couldn't care less. I just want to play ball in college and get the heck out of dull Westgate. You guys are lucky to be in Greeneville Heights."

Mason played with his coffee mug. "Actually, things are pretty rough in downtown Greeneville lately."

"Oh, yeah. Sorry to hear about all that."

"But your downtown seems to be on the upswing," Tessa said.

Danny's gaze slid from Mason to Tessa. "What's this really about, guys?"

Taking a deep breath, Tessa looked him squarely in the eyes. "Do you really know everything your dad is up to, Danny? Could he be involved in what is going on in Greeneville?"

Tessa was sure he would turn angry at her direct accusation, but he simply massaged his forehead and sighed. "I hope not, Tessa. But after what Troy did, who knows?" He leaned in to whisper, "My dad is a powerful guy in town, but his reach is expanding with the company. I used to keep my head down because I didn't want to know. But lately, I've been second-guessing everything."

"My dad brought your dad in for questioning recently. Did he tell you that?"

Danny's wide eyes proved that he didn't. "About the break-ins?" Tessa nodded, and the color drained from his face. "This is all making sense now."

"Sense?"

"I caught my dad taking a bunch of boxes from the file room. He never used to go in there. Way below his pay grade. But said he was just helping out." He dropped his head in his hand. "I really hope he wasn't destroying anything. This is such a mess."

Mason leaned forward and patted him on the shoulder. "Danny. None of this is your fault, regardless of what your dad might be doing."

"But we need to find out what he *is* doing," Tessa emphasized. "Especially if his plan is to devalue Greeneville's businesses and buy them up for a cheap price."

"You mean his real estate division?" Danny rubbed his forehead like it could somehow erase whatever plan his dad was concocting. He sat up as if snapping himself out of a funk. "What can I do to help?"

Tessa pursed her lips. She knew that even if Danny wanted to do the right thing, going against his father would be tough. Giving Mason another look, she pulled out a business card. "This is my dad's direct line at the station. He'll keep everything you say confidential, just like we will."

Danny silently took the card and nodded.

"Danny!" they heard from the coffee bar entrance as a man in an expensive dark pinstripe suit rushed over to them. Tessa's stomach twisted into several knots like a pretzel. She knew that face. She'd seen it several feet tall and all over Westgate—Dan Dunbar, *Senior.*

Tessa relaxed slightly seeing Danny carefully pocket her dad's business card. "Hey, Dad. Just chatting with some old friends."

An uncomfortable silence filled the space as everyone stood for the imposing business mogul. Tessa tried to embody Willow's phony demeanor with a fake grin. *You're all about facades anyway, Mr. Dunbar.*

"Aren't you the basketball guy?" Mr. Dunbar asked, pointing at Mason's face. "Yeah, the one who took the championship away from Troy." He shook his head of slicked-back hair to himself. "Such a pity about that foul call." Tessa cringed, watching his proximity to Mason while mocking his achievements.

Danny didn't seem to appreciate his dad's condescending tone either. "Dad. Mason was the MVP. He shot the winning basket." His eyes told Mason that he was sorry.

Mason offered his hand with a genuine smile. "Pleasure, sir." There was something striking about the way Mason could take the high road in any circumstance and remain charming. His calm demeanor was keeping Tessa from freaking out at the intimidating presence of Dan Dunbar.

"And who is this?" he asked, barely shaking Mason's hand, then moving on. "You look familiar too."

"Tessa's a runner, Dad. State Champion at Greeneville."

Mr. Dunbar used his pinkie finger, outfitted with a sparkling diamond ring, to point in Tessa's face. It wasn't only rude but clearly meant to intimidate her further. There was no question; he knew who she was. "I know. Tessa Wright. Your father is a Greeneville police detective." His own fake grin was nothing less than stomachache-inducing. "Tell me, Tessa. Is he Chief yet? I hear it's only a matter of time."

The closer Dan Dunbar got to Tessa, the closer Mason stood beside her. As brave as Tessa could be, she was grateful to have Mason there for backup. "Actually, he loves his job as *Lead* Detective. He's good at it. Perfect record. He likes to say he always gets his man."

"Humph," Mr. Dunbar said, his smile fading.

"Dad. Tessa and Mason said they need to get back. So, we shouldn't keep them."

Tessa involuntarily backed up the second the words left Danny's mouth. She was more than eager to get the heck out of there. Her job was done. She just hoped Danny could bring himself to help.

Resting his hand gently on Tessa's back, Mason said, "Good seeing you, Danny. We'll have to meet up on the court again sometime." Then, he turned to Mr. Dunbar. "Have a good day, sir." Inside, Tessa knew Mason was fuming.

They turned and started for the lobby when Dan Senior yelled, "Give my regards to your father, Tessa. Tell him I'll catch up with him someday soon. Real soon."

A shiver ran down her spine. It wasn't a friendly farewell; it was a warning. Tessa stole a glance over her shoulder at Danny and his fallen expression.

After pushing through the revolving door, Tessa rushed down the long, manicured walkway with pristine landscaping. When they'd finally reached the street, she collapsed onto the sidewalk, letting out a held breath. "Tessa, are you okay?"

Feeling sick, Tessa clutched her stomach. "He threatened my dad," she said, her voice quivering. "What if Danny doesn't want to help him?"

Mason scooped her off the ground and held her close. "Trust me, Tessa. He'll do the right thing."

"How do you know?"

"Because he's now seeing who his dad really is. And he doesn't want that to be him."

Chapter 20

Tessa slept horribly throughout the night, tossing and turning with visions of Dan Dunbar's gigantic head floating like a storm cloud over her. After several rounds of waking up amid the chirpy grumbles of Sherlock and Watson at her feet, she eventually drifted off before dawn.

It was nearly noon, the sun casting swaying leafy shadows on her turquoise walls, when she heard a knock on her door. "Come in," she said groggily through the fog of restless sleep.

Her mom peeked her head through the cracked door. "Tessa, I need to speak with you."

Snapping awake and upright, Tessa rubbed her eyes. Dr. Wright's voice meant business.

"Yeah, Mom?" she said, trying to sound alert.

She expected her mom to sit beside her on the bed. However, as Tessa lifted her tired eyes, Dr. Wright was still standing in her scrubs. "Tessa, you need to get ready as soon as you can. I'm dropping you off at the station on my way to the office."

"What's wrong?" she asked, her throat abruptly closing up.

Her mom leaned against the door jamb. "Your dad called. He wants you to stop by."

Rubbing her forehead, Tessa couldn't remember the last time she'd seen her dad for more than a few minutes at a time in recent weeks. He was always at the station or getting a paltry amount of sleep late at night. "Did he say why?"

"Just please get dressed, Tessa. You can work it out with him." Tessa started trembling all over. Her dad was usually a teddy bear, despite his tough Marine and police backgrounds. But even her easygoing mom now seemed a tad uptight. An overall air of dread hung heavy in the room.

"Sure, Mom. I'll be ready in ten," she said, throwing off her covers and heading for the bathroom.

Nine and a half minutes later, Tessa breezed by Hanna in the kitchen, who was cheerfully feeding Cam in a highchair. Even their housekeeper seemed to sense that something was off, and she patted Tessa on the back before placing a shiny red apple in her hand.

Without a word, Tessa started for the garage, where her mom was already waiting in the driver's side of the SUV. The atmosphere was so intense during the car ride that Tessa didn't even have the courage to ask if she was actually in trouble. But her confused emotions, bubbling at the surface, seemed on the verge of boiling over when Dr. Wright pulled into the police station parking lot. No one in their right mind would feel comfortable in a police station, except Tessa. Well, except today.

"Thanks for the ride, Mom," she murmured, fumbling for the door handle with sweaty palms. To her surprise, her mom reached over and gave her a kiss on the cheek.

Keeping her focus on the entrance, Tessa couldn't bring herself to look back at her mom. She clutched the red apple tightly in her hand and swallowed back a lump in her throat as she pushed into the bustling station.

Tessa wasn't used to being here on a Sunday afternoon. That was a time usually reserved for her agency meetings. And then, she remembered—her meeting. Pulling out her cell phone, she typed a quick text, canceling the meeting. *Family stuff,* she wrote, but even she didn't know what that meant.

She was familiar with the layout of the station and quickly bypassed Patty at the reception desk. Even on a Sunday, the station was thick with uniformed and plain-clothes officers milling about and manning desks. After the string of break-ins consumed the capacity of the force, Tessa's dad acquired additional funding to hire more hands. At that very moment, she felt like she was seeing them all in front of her eyes. *All hands on deck.*

Instead of the usual pleasant expressions and cordial smiles, everyone's heads were down, consumed by the work on their desks. Even when she passed Bobby Warren, his favorite Boston Red Sox coffee mug was empty. His grinning face was replaced with a serious and determined expression as he sifted through a tall stack of files, never looking up to greet her with his usual, "Hey, runnah." Something was off, no question, and that sense of dread was returning with a vengeance.

Despite the loud sounds of chatter, ringing phones, and general office noise, Tessa tiptoed to the back toward her dad's large office. She hesitated, listening through the door. Was his normally calm voice angry or elevated? But all she heard from the other side was silence. Maybe that was worse. Lightly tapping the wood door, Tessa was partially hoping there would be no answer. But a firm "Come in" was the response, and her heart pounded against her ribs. She wondered if he could hear it all the way from behind the door.

Tessa's palms were so sweaty, she could barely turn the handle. When she finally mustered the courage to enter, she halted only inches from the doorway and studied her dad. He was slumped over his desk, his face showing months of exhaustion and frustration. As he raised his blue eyes, dimmed from fatigue, she could barely meet his gaze. "Hi, Dad," she said so softly it was almost inaudible.

He waved her in and pointed to one of the upholstered chairs across from his desk. "Sit, Tessa."

This is so not good, she thought, wiping her clammy palms on her jeans.

Detective Wright was quiet as he finished some paperwork, then silenced his cell phone. Tessa wasn't about to rush him. Putting off whatever was coming was far superior to enduring it. Instead, she stared at her perfect apple, cradled in her quivering hands.

After what seemed like forever and also only seconds, her dad rounded his desk and sat in the chair beside her. "Are you going to eat that?" he asked, pointing to her apple.

Tessa answered with a silent shrug.

Sighing, Detective Wright rubbed his eyes and forehead. "Well, I had a very interesting morning."

"Oh?" was all Tessa said, still staring at the apple.

"Yes. A visitor came in. First thing. Very eager."

Tessa simply nodded, her gaze apple-focused.

"Danny Dunbar. But that isn't a surprise to you, is it, Tessa?"

Closing her eyes, she cringed. *Actually, it is a surprise, Dad. I didn't know if he'd really do it.* When she lifted her chin to meet his gaze, she couldn't seem to read her dad's expression. Was he angry, amused, curious, or a combination thereof? Was this some kind of "good cop" interrogation technique? Regardless, Tessa still didn't feel compelled to speak.

So, Detective Wright continued as he relaxed back into his chair and crossed his arms. His Marine Corps tattoo was slightly visible from the rolled-up sleeve of his dress shirt. "Danny brought a whole slew of interesting things. Files, emails on a flash drive, even his own notes." Then, he leaned forward, his blue eyes serious and unwavering. "Seems he was clued in about his dad's real estate business. The one that's been buying up depreciated properties several towns over. And the more Danny looked into it, the worse it got."

Tessa's dad stood and lifted some files off his desk. "Not too long ago, I talked with Dan Senior—or tried at least—for three hours and got nothing. The guy was clean as a whistle. But somehow, I now have more evidence to comb through than I know what to do with." He thrust his chin toward the door. "All those men and women out there are working on it." Detective Wright rounded his desk again and sat across from his daughter. "I have conspiracy and fraud of the highest magnitude, Tessa. Felonies everywhere. And this guy hid it all. Even from his family."

The sick feeling in Tessa's stomach was returning, especially when she considered Danny's future. But even his younger brother Troy would suffer as a result of his dad's malfeasance.

"How did you do it, Tessa?" She bit her lip. Did she even need to answer? Her dad obviously knew how. Danny must have said so. But he leaned in closer. "Talk to me, Tessa."

"He just decided to do the right thing," was her simple answer.

Detective Wright sighed and sank into his chair. "You knew how dangerous that was, going to Dunbar's home base. I told you so, and you didn't listen."

Tessa braced herself. She knew all of this was coming. How she had directly disobeyed his warnings. And the worst part was, deep down, she knew he was right. Dan Dunbar was a bad guy and something bad could have happened to her or—even worse—to Mason. "I'm sorry, Dad."

He reached for her hand and squeezed it. "Do you have any idea how difficult it is being Tessa Wright's dad?"

"Um." She had no idea what to say to that. Was she really that bad of a daughter? "If you want to ground me ..."

"That's not what I meant. I have no idea what to do with you, Tessa. You single-handedly solved this thing, put yourself on the line to get the evidence, and did it all by the book." He held up the stack of files again with his free hand. "All this evidence that Danny provided is admissible. He even started contacting witnesses to come in. We're scheduling them as we speak." Tessa was at a loss for words. "You did the right thing and convinced someone else to do the same. What the heck am I supposed to do with that?"

Tessa had no idea. All she knew was that someone was doing something very wrong, and it was hurting those she cared about the most—the people of Greenville Heights. She knew she had to stop it.

"I'll tell you what we're going to do ..." Tessa braced herself again when she heard a knock on the door. "Yup. Come in."

"Hey, boss," Bobby said cheerfully. Tessa could smell it before she saw it as the room filled with the familiar scents of garlic, oregano, and fresh basil. Bobby was carrying a Tony's pizza box and paper bag, which she could only assume held the most prized item of all—garlic knots. "Hey, runnah," he added, dropping the box and bag on the desk and offering Tessa a high-five.

"I appreciate it, Bobby," Detective Wright said, lifting the top of the box. "Take one for the road. Great job out there."

"Thanks, boss." He stole a large slice of pepperoni and was already devouring it on his way out the door.

Tessa's dad placed a slice on a paper plate and handed it to her. "What's this?" she asked with a dumbfounded stare at the plate.

"This is lunch. We're gonna eat and talk about all of this. Step by step."

Tessa hesitated, absorbing his words, then eagerly took the plate. "Um, thanks."

Detective Wright grabbed a slice for himself and dropped a garlic knot onto his daughter's plate. "So, I want to hear all about your meet yesterday and how you conveniently *did not* take the bus back with your team." His stern gaze was not lost on her. "Then, you're going to tell me every detail about visiting Dunbar Enterprises."

"You got it, Dad," she said, munching on her garlic knot.

"And … you are going to share some more about this boy-friend of yours." Tessa took a hard swallow. This grilling was going to be worse than anything about Dan Dunbar.

"Oh? What do you want to know?"

Her dad leaned over his desk, never blinking. "I want to know all about this guy who seems to care for my daughter quite a lot, Tessa. Enough to have your back against the likes of Dan Dunbar."

Chapter 21

As Tessa strolled downtown Greeneville Heights two weeks later, both autumn and Halloween were visible on every corner of bustling Main Street. She happily dodged strollers and dog walkers amid the ghosts and goblins hanging from streetlamps and outside of businesses. With a slight chill in the air, she hugged her track jacket and her *Nancy Drew* novel close to her chest as she kicked around a few stray crumpled leaves on her way to the library.

Tessa passed Gus's, where customers spilled onto the sidewalk from his outdoor seating during Sunday brunch hour. Raising her nose, she smelled the spicy and sweet aromas of the best chicken and waffles for miles. She paused in front of Sue Ann's salon to wave through her large picture window. In a couple of days, she'd be sitting in one of those leather chairs, finally attending to her unruly hair. All around Tessa, street trees swayed back and forth in the breeze, their leaves giving a subtle hint of the fall color explosion to come.

Arriving at the library, Tessa took a deep inhale of refreshing autumn air, her head tilted back to the cornflower-blue sky. It reminded her of the blue cloth of the vintage novel she was about to return. She was sad to let it go, but grateful to be entrusted with it at all.

When she entered the brick building this time, it was packed with patrons hovering over the long tables and milling about the dusty colorful shelves. It was just as a library should be— occupied and enjoyed. Even the circulation desk was busy, and Tessa didn't mind patiently waiting in line, especially if it gave her more precious minutes with her book.

Through the bobbing heads around her, Linda noticed Tessa and waved her up. "Good afternoon! What a wonderful surprise." The friendly librarian was always pleased to see Tessa, but she seemed especially upbeat today. Unfolding her arms, Tessa presented the book to Linda. But before she had a chance to say anything, the librarian pushed a copy of the *Greeneville Gazette* toward her. "Congratulations are in order."

Tessa beamed, her gaze moving to the crisp Sunday edition of the local newspaper. She assumed Linda was referring to the huge sports spread on her latest cross-country meet, where Greeneville was once again the victor, and she had earned another individual gold medal (her fourth of the season). Instead, she pointed to the front page's enormous headline: "Dunbar's Downfall." Nodding, Tessa couldn't help but appreciate the clever alliteration.

"Yeah. My dad is really proud of his team. I guess Dunbar's going away for a while."

Linda cupped her hand and whispered, "Thanks to you. We all know you helped." She winked and offered the paper to Tessa.

Tessa took a hard swallow, her mouth as dry as the Sahara. She knew the rumor mill ran rampant in town, but she and her dad had been very careful. As far as they were concerned, Danny Dunbar came forward of his own volition and for his own conscience. "Thanks," Tessa said uncomfortably.

And when she once again offered Linda the book, the cheerful librarian waved it away. "Keep it. I can think of no better owner."

Tessa's sapphire eyes widened. "But … are you sure?"

"Absolutely. This town owes you one. Look at how things have changed." She outstretched her arms at the busy scene around her, then placed the paper and the book in the young sleuth's hands with a wink.

When Tessa waltzed out of the library, there was a bit more spring in her already-chipper step. She checked the time on the clock tower over City Hall, then slid onto a wooden bench under a shady oak tree. Unfurling the newspaper, she skimmed past the headline and dived into the details.

In the end, Dan Dunbar Senior was running a criminal enterprise, not a business one. His successful delivery business, which started as legitimate, turned into a front—for the break-ins in Greeneville Heights. Entrusted with keys and security codes to allow for deliveries on and off-hours, the perpetrators were able to access the buildings. The crimes scared the downtown patrons so severely, Greeneville's Main Street was dying.

Rex Jamison was implicated as someone on the "inside." Apparently, stealing bikes and skateboards was only the tip of his criminal iceberg (especially when he could easily swipe a few bucks out of Chuck Murphy's antique register as a bonus).

And Dunbar didn't stop there. Once he saw towns like Greeneville suffering, he'd jump in as their savior, arguing that he was rescuing failed handfuls of businesses by buying them up at very low prices. But that was where his fake generosity ended. He'd use his financial gains for his own deteriorating downtown in Westgate, hoping the upscale appearance would bring in more traffic to his other businesses. And the cycle continued.

Some businesses were tired of Dunbar's bullying as he pushed new contracts on owners that they couldn't refuse or when he offered to buy them up but they failed to cave (like Davies Deliveries). Tessa's eyes moved to the lamppost beside her and the bright flyer advertising bike deliveries by "Davies." Dunbar tried to squash them, and they wouldn't give up. Now that Dunbar was through, they were thriving.

Then, Tessa's thoughts went to Danny. Mason had kept in touch with him as they'd given their support. Danny didn't want to be anyone's hero. He was heartbroken that his father could do such horrible things. Even his not-so-squeaky-clean brother Troy was beyond embarrassed and keeping a low profile. But Tessa could see Danny as the bright light in a dark tunnel, with his focus on returning to the Westgate Warriors high school basketball team. Westgate needed a guy like Danny Dunbar. Incidentally, he was contemplating dropping the "Dunbar" and using his mother's maiden name instead.

Hopping off the bench, Tessa straightened the "Davies Deliveries" advertisement, then noticed the Astronomy Society's shimmering flyer about the upcoming meteor shower. Riley was right. It did sound like a fun night under the stars at Greeneville's beautiful park and the perfect way for the town to celebrate its revitalization—new beginnings all around.

With a skip in her step, Tessa hurried down the block. When she saw Mason relaxing against a street tree in front of Lorraine's, her heart sped up with her feet. Mason was sporting his evergreen basketball sweatshirt, his downward gaze focused on his cell phone. Combing his fingers through his dark waves, he looked up in time to catch Tessa approaching. Immediately, his face lit up as his eyes reflected the afternoon sun's orange rays.

"Were you waiting long?" Tessa asked, reaching for a hug.

"Nah. Just enjoying the day." His gaze drifted to her book, tucked between the *Gazette*. "I thought you were stopping at the library."

"Actually, Linda kind of gifted it to me."

"Wow. Another reason to celebrate."

Mason held open the door for Tessa, and it was like they'd stepped through time. The jukebox was throwing out a 1950s hit to the jam-packed diner. Everyone's favorite waitress, Molly, waved them to the last booth available in the corner, and Tessa slid in and relaxed into the turquoise and red cushions. "Shakes?" Molly asked without prompting, and they nodded.

They didn't even bother to open the menu. Tessa had memorized it anyway. She'd been going to Lorraine's since she was a little kid. "Are you excited for your first game next week?" The start of Mason's basketball season was quickly approaching with an exhibition game on Saturday.

"Yeah. Can't wait. Sorry about your last meet. I probably can catch the end, depending on your wave." Tessa's last cross-country meet of the regular season was also on Saturday and finally at home in Greeneville Heights. Unfortunately, it directly conflicted with Mason's game.

"That's okay. But whose idea was it to schedule every-thing at the same time?" She shook her head to herself as Molly returned with the shakes.

"Anything else, guys?" she asked.

"The Combo, please. And some onion rings," he said, and she rushed off without even writing down their usual order. Then, Mason held up his shake glass. "To both of us, and our A-worthy essays."

Tessa giggled as they clinked glasses. Like last time, Tessa and Mason had earned the same grades on their essays, ending their bet in a tie. But, unlike last time, Tessa didn't question if this excursion was just for the bet or a real date. It was both.

"What's with the paper? Checking out the cross-coun-try spread?"

Opening it up, Tessa tapped the front page. "Big headline."

"Yeah. My dad's got a lot of work ahead of him with the trial, like your dad."

Tessa's eyes remained on the front-page photo of Dan Dunbar. "They took down all those billboards in Westgate. It's like they're trying to erase him from their town's history."

"They can try all they want, but no one is going to for-get anytime soon." She nodded, playing with her hands. "What's wrong?" he asked, nudging her.

"I just feel bad for Danny."

Mason put his arm around her. "He'll be okay, Tessa. He knows he did the right thing."

Molly returned and dropped off a large burger, cut in half, with curly fries and a plate of steaming onion rings, ranch dressing on the side. Mason pushed the onion rings toward Tessa. "Ladies first."

"So," Tessa said, dunking a ring into the dressing. "Are we certain about our costumes for the Halloween party?"

"Are you asking if I'm okay with *your* suggestion?" Mason started on his half of the burger.

"Well, it would be a *couple's* thing." Tessa aimlessly swirled a fry in ketchup, waiting for Mason's answer.

Tapping her playfully on the nose, Mason leaned close. "Seeing as we're a couple, I'm game."

Tessa kissed him on the cheek. "I was hoping you'd say that."

Chapter 22

You have *got* to be kidding me," Tessa said, surrounded by a field of deep mud craters. While the clearing sky above indicated a better day ahead, the scene around her revealed the mess of weather that had transpired overnight. *Rain—lots of rain.* And the area around Greeneville Heights Middle School was a mess because of it. Although reminiscent of cross-country tryouts, Tessa still was not a fan.

"Maybe it will dry out," Riley said in a hopeful voice.

Tessa shot her a side-eye, lifting her spikes up from the muck. "In a half hour? I almost prefer the bugs," she mumbled.

Riley raised an eyebrow, then offered a sympathetic look as Coach Powers called her team to huddle up.

A general annoyance over the condition of the field swept across the group. Even Nick and Owen were rolling their eyes when Coach Powers pointed out the particularly "rough turns" on the challenging course. For Tessa, massive anxiety was setting in. She never really felt comfortable in muddy conditions. They were pretty much the exact opposite of her sleek track. And after a long season of endurance running, her legs were already beyond spent.

To make matters worse, Greeneville was slated for the final wave in this huge meet. More foot traffic over the muddy terrain and the course was bound to be an absolute disaster by the time Tessa had to traverse it.

As some ominous clouds rolled in, blocking the warm, dry sun, Tessa hugged her singlet against her petite frame. A cool breeze kicked up and lifted her hair, held back by a sports headband. She sighed at the cozy, brightly lit school building in the distance. Mason was inside playing his first game, and she couldn't help but wish she were there instead of freezing her butt off in a field of mud.

"Something tells me we've seen the last of the sun for today," Owen said, tilting his head back at the menacing sky.

"Tell me about it," Tessa groaned.

Owen studied her apprehensive expression. "You'll be great, track star. Just watch that last turn around the hill. It's a pretty steep slide down if you miss."

Tessa nodded, remembering Coach Powers' warning. "I just want to get this over with."

As they trudged to the start area, weaving around the especially slick spots, Owen slung his arm around her. "I got your back, Tessa. Remember to dig in and don't be intimidated by the mud."

When Tessa took in the view around her, it was hard not to be intimidated. While River Valley had started in the previous wave, Greeneville was still up against the likes of Avondale in their own. As a mass of green and brown singlets pushed to the front, Tessa felt a tap behind her. Glancing over her shoulder, she expected to see Riley and Nick. Instead, Amelia waved shyly. "Good luck, Tessa," she said.

"You too, Amelia. Oh, and be careful …"

"Around the last curve, right?"

Tessa gave her a wink before putting her game face on. To her left, Nick had already done so, while Riley appeared as uneasy as Tessa felt.

"Good luck with the mud," Tessa whispered to Riley.

"I'm not worried about that. I'm worried about Carly and Amelia."

Amid shouts of encouragement from their coaches, the last wave of the day in the last cross-country meet of the regular season began. Despite her worries, within the first loop in the four-loop course, Tessa was neck and neck with Amelia out front. Nick and Owen were also vying for first, although Owen was having an easier time with the muddy course. By the second loop, Tessa was already covered in mud up to her knees and was sure she would be wearing it in her hair by the time she finished. But she had pushed past Amelia and seemed to be running the course solo, with no one in sight. As Tessa started the third loop, raindrops began to fall from the one massive gray cloud directly overhead. She groaned but kept going, very much looking forward to the finish chute.

In fact, Tessa's mind was so consumed by the thought of finishing that she wasn't paying attention to her footing as she rounded the last sharp turn. Focusing ahead and not down, she planted her right foot in a slick mud crater, twisting her ankle. "Ouch!" she shouted, completely losing her balance and sliding down the steep hill. For a few scary seconds, Tessa didn't know which way was up as she rolled end-over-end down the embankment, ultimately landing at the foot of a tall pine in a large cluster of trees.

With only her ragged breathing and the distant trickle of the lake to keep her company, she tried to grasp exactly what had happened. Scrutinizing her appearance, Tessa found she was covered in mud and leaves from head to toe. Her right foot, the source of the issue, was freezing cold. And it was obvious why; her shoe was completely missing, probably lost in a mud crater on her less-than-graceful descent down the embankment. After catching her breath, Tessa pushed herself fully upright with the help of the sturdy pine tree behind her. "Yes!" she cheered, feeling victorious just to be standing. But the moment she tried to walk on her ankle, she winced. "Shoot!"

Tessa concentrated on the tall hill she had to climb to get back on the course. Mere seconds before, she was only worried about her placement at the finish line. Now, she was worried about getting to the finish at all. *You can do this, Tessa. Shoe or no shoe. You have to.*

Sheer determination, or Tessa grit, pulled her up the steep hill by her knees. Gulping down some air, she peered over the top, hoping to signal the first person she saw. She waited, starting to shiver, then gratefully spotted a figure approaching. Her heart sank, noticing the singlet was brown and not green. But as the person approached, her hopes lifted. Waving frantically, she yelled, "Amelia!"

The tiny Avondale runner's face lost all color when she saw Tessa. Skidding to a stop, she said, "Tessa, what happened?" Then, her eyes fell on something near her, and she seemed to know. "Is this your shoe?"

"Oh, thank you!" Tessa said, taking her missing spikes. But, as she tried to slip it on her caked-on foot, it wouldn't budge. *No chance finishing this race now unless I crawl through the finish chute.*

As Tessa attempted to pull herself up over the embankment, Amelia reached down, giving her a hand. "Let me help." But the two tiny girls were no match for a slick, muddy hill, and Tessa slid even farther down.

"It's okay, Amelia. You go and finish. You could win this thing."

Amelia's eyes grew as wide as saucers. "No way I'm leaving you, Tessa."

Tessa protested again, but Amelia's gaze was drawn behind her in the distance. She jumped up and waved. "Help!"

As Tessa dropped her head in her muddy hand, the last thing she wanted was to bring another runner down with her. "Amelia, it's ok ..." And then, she saw Owen approaching in his green singlet. When he spotted the scene, he sprinted toward them.

"Tessa, are you okay?"

She tried to contain her relieved emotions at seeing Owen. "Yeah." And when she simply held up her shoe, he understood.

Turning to Amelia, he said, "Go and finish. We'll meet you there."

"Thanks," Tessa said, when Amelia had disappeared. Maybe she could still place well, especially in these conditions.

"Can you stand?" he asked, staring down at Tessa on her knees on the edge of the hill.

"Yeah. Just can't get my shoe on."

Owen reached down to help her up. "Thank goodness you're tiny, track star."

His teasing calmed the tense situation, making her almost forget her uncomfortable predicament. But when Tessa stepped forward to boost herself up, her face twisted into a wince. "Ouch," she hissed.

"Are you hurt?" he asked, pointing to her ankle.

"I'm okay. You should just go and finish."

Owen gave her a look like she was crazy. "Tessa, I'm not leaving a hurt teammate."

Tears welled in her eyes, and she lowered her face to hide them. "I shouldn't be the reason you lose."

"I'm gonna lose anyway. Nick has probably already finished. A DNF won't matter. And Mason would kick my butt if he knew I left his girlfriend in a ditch— rightfully so too."

As Tessa smiled weakly, a tear rolled down her cheek. "Thanks."

"Okay. I know you're as strong as steel, Tessa Wright, but will you please allow me to pull you up and carry you? Or we'll never get out of this mud pit."

"Yes," she said with a soft chuckle.

Owen scooped her up as more runners passed by, staring at them like a car wreck. And, when the pair approached the finish chute, filled with spectators, coaches, and volunteers, it turned into even more of a spectacle. Coach Powers and some volunteers with medical gear ran in their direction. "This is seriously embarrassing," Tessa whispered to Owen.

"You think this scene is bad, you should see how you *look*. You're absolutely covered in mud."

"The story of my life," she mumbled. "Better than bugs, I guess."

"Whatever you say, track star."

But Tessa's embarrassment turned into relief once again when she saw her mom and dad. "What happened?" Dr. Wright shouted while Owen gently set Tessa on the ground.

The next several minutes went by in a blur as Tessa was surrounded by helping hands and onlookers. She was grateful that Owen and Amelia were there to squash the continued questioning. Eventually, Dr. Wright whispered something to Tessa's dad and Coach Powers, then declared, "We're taking her to my office for examination. She's freezing out here." Then, she turned to Owen. "Would you mind helping me get her to the car?"

Before Owen scooped her up yet again, Tessa whispered to Nick, "Take care of Riley, okay?" gesturing toward her teary-eyed best friend.

"You got it," he said, patting her on the shoulder.

"This is a disaster," Tessa said into her hand as Owen carried her to her parents' SUV. Then, as they passed the illuminated school building, bursting with activity, she added, "Could you let Mason know what happened? Um, but *after* his game."

Owen gave a simple nod. "Well, track star, this is for sure my most memorable meet ever."

Chapter 23

By the time Tessa's dad carried her into an examination room in her mom's office, she was visibly shivering. Part of it was due to the cold mud covering her every limb. But, as the initial adrenaline wore off, the severity of the situation dawned on her. While Tessa sat alone in the room dotted with baby safari animals on the walls, she stared at her ankle and tried to hold back tears. This wasn't about not finishing a race or even not winning it; it could mean the end of her track career.

As tears finally poured down her cheeks, she slapped the examination table in frustration. *Why did I have to do cross-country?* Of course, it was a silly thing to be angry about. Up until this point, she was on her way to another state title. But Tessa knew she didn't love it as much as track. And to think her first love might be taken away was a hard pill to swallow.

She was still gulping back tears with her hand over her face when her mom rushed inside with a blanket. "Oh, sweetie. It's gonna be okay," she said, wrapping up her trembling daughter.

"Is … it … really … bad?" she asked as her teeth chattered. Moments like these, she was glad her mom was a physician. When Tessa was little, her mom always knew which fever was a serious one, how to properly wrap up a cut, and if it really required stitches. Now, Tessa needed Dr. Wright's reassurance not as her daughter, but as an athlete.

Her mom wiped her damp cheeks. "I won't know until I examine you, sweetie. We'll do X-rays just in case, and I'll send them off to the best radiologist I know. Then, we can talk with an orthopedist too, if necessary. Okay?"

Tessa nodded, but more tears rained down.

Dr. Wright went to work, cleaning and examining Tessa's ankle. Thankfully, it was only slightly swollen and bruised. After several X-rays, Tessa's mom wrapped it up tightly in an ACE bandage while her daughter waited with bated breath. "Well, nothing appears broken, and there's no indication that you've torn any ligaments or tendons."

Tessa was so overjoyed, she would have leapt off the table, if she could.

"However, I left a message with an orthopedist, Dr. Lawrence, asking for a consult. We'll see if he suggests an MRI as well."

Sitting up with trepidation, Tessa asked softly, "So, what does that mean?"

Dr. Wright took a seat beside her and brushed some hair off her face. "It means that for today, you rest, ice and elevate it, and keep it wrapped. And … I'll give you a pair of crutches to use."

"Mom!" *Crutches are the worst. Crutches mean I'm injured.*

"Tessa, it's only for a couple of days. Even if it's just a slight sprain, it will heal faster if you stay off it completely."

So, it was official. Maybe her track career wasn't over. But her cross-country one was, at least her middle school one. The competitive athlete in Tessa was heartbroken.

Wiping tears off her cheeks, Tessa nodded. She knew this was non-negotiable. "Can I have a minute?"

"Yes, sweetie. I'll grab the crutches. But I do have a packed waiting room, with lots of people wanting to see you."

"Mom, I don't want to see anyone. Can you just tell them I'm okay?"

Dr. Wright stood and gently patted her arm. "All right. But Mason's here, still in his basketball uniform. I think he's wearing a hole in my floor, pacing."

"It's embarrassing, Mom."

She sighed. "Tessa, it's not embarrassing when people who care about you worry."

"Fine. I'll see Mason, even though I look like a mess."

"Something tells me he's not going to care about that, sweetie."

Tessa spent the next few minutes composing herself, despite incessant tears falling. She almost slipped off the table when she heard a soft knock. "Come in."

A set of apprehensive green eyes peeked through the crack in the door. "You sure?"

Taking a deep breath, she waved him in. "It's not my best day, though."

When Mason stepped inside wearing his sweatshirt over his uniform, Tessa was sure he had left the court in a hurry. His dark, wavy hair was disheveled, and he had an overall look of defeat. Tessa's best guess was that he appeared very, very worried. He loitered near the threshold, hugging the door uncomfortably. "Are you all right?" he eventually asked, inching himself closer.

It was an easy question, but she didn't know how to answer it. If anyone else had asked it, she would have said "yes." But somehow Mason was different. So, she shook her head and more tears flowed with a vengeance. "I'm sorry," she mumbled between sobs.

Mason pulled her into a tight embrace. "Everything will work out, Tessa."

"But I messed it all up. The race. The season. My team."

"Tessa, you've been bringing up your whole team all season. Owen even said so. Sometimes you gotta let your team bring you up."

Nodding between sniffles, Tessa slowly pulled away. "Did you win?"

Mason's face lit up. "Yup. By eight points. Owen was waiting for me before I went to the locker room."

"Sorry. Guess I would have been bad luck today."

"Nah. You're always good luck, Tessa."

Her cheeks were still burning when her mom returned with the crutches. "I'm trusting Mason to make sure you don't ditch these at school."

Tessa suppressed a *groan* until her mom walked back out. "This is gonna suck."

"It won't be too bad," Mason said, wrapping his arm around her. "I can walk you to all your classes now."

Without warning, a loud rapping came from the door. "Come in," Tessa said, rolling her eyes.

"Tessa!" was heard as friendly faces filled the room, including Leah, Skylar, Nick, and Caleb. Riley's tear-stained cheeks were replaced with relief, probably just glad her best friend wasn't sporting a cast. Amelia slowly came in, and Tessa noticed her silver medal. *Carly is surely wearing a gold.*

Even Owen waltzed in and announced, "See? Totally memorable day, track star."

Tessa laughed, testing her crutches as everyone cheered her on like she was a baby taking her first steps. It wasn't exactly how she had planned to remember the day, but she had to admit, it was one that she wouldn't soon forget.

Chapter 24

Halloween night had arrived, and Tessa was admiring her reflection in her bedroom's full-length mirror. Staring back at her was a 1940s blue knit dress with three-quarter sleeves, coordinating belt, and adorable front pockets that she had gotten from Cleo's vintage section. Of course, due to her recent cross-country mishap, she had to forgo the matching dress shoes for the comfort of her Keds.

Glancing at the discarded crutches leaning against the wall, she was thrilled to ditch them for the evening as she sported only an ACE bandage. Thankfully, Tessa was ultimately diagnosed with a mild ankle sprain. Although she had to end her cross-country season early, the doctors and Coach Linden were confident that she'd be healed and in top form by the time her track team resumed practices in the spring.

But her most noticeable change in appearance was accomplished with the help of Sue Ann's very skilled hands and several hours at her salon. When Tessa heard the *ring* of the doorbell downstairs, her body tingled with anticipation for Mason to see the results.

"Good evening, Mason. That's quite a new look," Detective Wright said, answering the door as Tessa gingerly made her way down the stairs. She could walk without any discomfort, but (ever the doctor) her mom still had suggested she take it easy, especially tonight.

"It's a costume party, Dad," Tessa reminded him before he dashed into the kitchen.

"Let me know when you're ready to go," he said over his shoulder with a wink, prepared to be their chauffeur to Huntington Manor.

Mason's green eyes sparkled, and his jaw dropped to the floor when he saw her. Tessa was just as floored with his vintage appearance, including his trimmed dark waves that were casually slicked back. He wore a powder-blue pullover sweater and brown slacks, all from Cleo's 1940s section. With his height and athletic physique, Mason was the perfect Ned Nickerson to Tessa's Nancy Drew. "You look awesome," she said.

"And you look …" Mason cupped some curls in her new short bob. Not only did she have a new do, but Sue Ann had meticulously highlighted it. With Tessa's natural reds coming through her chestnut mane, she was now a true auburn. And she adorned it with a matching blue ribbon for an extra vintage touch.

But with Mason appearing dumbfounded, worry seeped into Tessa's thoughts. "It's okay, right?"

Mason smiled broadly. "It's perfect. You look so … pretty."

Tessa was speechless. In the back of her mind, she'd hoped Mason thought she was pretty but had never heard him say the actual words. "Thank you," she said when she finally found her voice.

"So, are you ready to check out a haunted house?" he asked, reaching for her hand.

"Depends," she said, grabbing the special addition to her costume—her vintage *Nancy Drew* book. "Are *you ready* for some sleuthing?"

"Do you even have to ask?"

Tessa was about to call her dad when her mom ran into the foyer with a baby bottle in her hand. "Wait. Wait. Wait," she said breathlessly. "I want to take some photos."

"With that?" Tessa joked, pointing to the bottle.

Dr. Wright rolled her eyes. "Oh, good grief. Hold on." Running back into the kitchen, she retrieved her camera, then snapped several photos of the couple. "You two look fantastic."

"Your chariot awaits," Tessa's dad said, spinning the key fob between his fingers.

A few minutes later, when they arrived at Riley's mom's house, Tessa scoffed at her best friend's costume. "Your track warm-ups? Really?"

"I couldn't think of anything. And it's not too bad since it's still cross-country season. Plus, we're lucky my parents even said I could go."

"Fine. Are we picking up Nick next?"

Riley scrunched up her face and hid behind her glasses. "Um, I kinda didn't ask him. Just said I'd see him there."

Tessa stared at her friend with her mouth agape. "What? You chickened out?" Groaning, she pulled Riley out of the house before her mom decided to change her mind.

"Mason looks really cute," Riley whispered, giggling as they slid into the back seat.

"I know, right?"

A little while later, Detective Wright dropped them off in front of Huntington Manor. All the activity around the house indicated that a massive bash was happening inside. On the outside, the old Victorian still gave off an incredibly creepy aura, especially on Halloween.

"Wow. A full moon and Huntington Manor," Riley whispered with apprehension. "We must be crazy."

Tessa sighed. "It's not a real haunted house. I'm sure there's a logical explanation."

"Hey, guys!" they heard as Leah bounded toward them, dressed as an artist's palette, down to the actual paint splotches all over and her life-sized paintbrush.

"Now, that's a costume," Tessa said, shooting a side-eye at Riley.

Mason seemed thoroughly impressed. "Did you really make that?"

Leah spun around, modeling her costume. "Yup. Every bit of it." Then, she took in the sleuthing couple and nudged Tessa. "That is so perfect, especially for tonight."

"Where's Sky?" Tessa asked.

Leah performed a massive eye roll. "Inside, following Ethan around. Just look for the trail of glitter."

The group made its way up the uneven sidewalk, toward the rickety front steps, and past a fake graveyard with spooky soundtrack and lighting. When a guy dressed up like a vampire jumped out of a coffin, Riley freaked out and had to grab Leah's paintbrush to keep from falling down the steps. Tessa sighed and shrugged it off.

Once inside, the music was deafening. Leah waved Riley into another room where she'd spotted Nick. "See you guys later," she yelled over her shoulder.

"You want something to drink?" Mason shouted, and Tessa chuckled. "What?"

"Why do we always end up at places where we can't even talk?"

They headed for a long table, covered with an orange and black tablecloth and placed beneath a dimmed chandelier draped in fake spiderwebs. "Wow. They really went all out," Mason said, pointing to the Halloween-themed treats and punch bowls. "Pick your poison, I guess?"

"I'll take the orange one," she said, choosing the foamy concoction immersed in foggy dry ice.

"You sure?" He gestured toward the other deep red punch bowl filled with what appeared to be bobbing fake eyeballs.

Tessa stuck out her tongue and he laughed.

As they were enjoying their punch, Tessa's gaze caught a lot of sparkle and she understood exactly what Leah was talking about. Skylar was outfitted in her *Falconettes* dance team uniform. But she'd kicked it up several notches, covering her face in evergreen and silver glittery makeup and wrapping up her long, blonde hair in a sequined bow. Her evergreen top was tied a bit higher and tighter. She even carried her crinkly pompoms as she trailed Ethan, simply dressed in his basketball uniform. "What is with everyone just wearing their uniforms?" Tessa groaned.

Mason gave her an uneasy look. "I'm not an expert, but I don't think that's really Skylar's uniform."

Tessa had to agree. Skylar clearly had upped her outfit for Ethan's benefit. But Tessa felt uneasy herself, scouring the space for the host. "Where is Willow?"

"There you are, Greene!" Caleb yelled to Mason through the loud techno music. "Lookin' good. Very vintage."

The guys bumped fists as Tessa tried to hold back another *groan* at Caleb's sad excuse for a costume. "Your basketball uniform? Did you guys just come as the team?"

Caleb beamed. "Not just the basketball team, but the *championship-winning* basketball team." He held up his jersey with a patch on the front as proof.

Still not impressed, Tessa leaned into Mason's ear. "I'm gonna try to find Willow."

Wandering around Huntington Manor was less spooky and more cringeworthy, as Tessa encountered costumes that ranged from gory to goofy. When she spotted a tall blonde with a flowing white dress, she made a beeline in her direction, but was suddenly grabbed from behind. "Tessa Wright!" the girl said, adjusting her pointy witch's hat.

"Um, yeah." Tessa thought she might look familiar, but the green face paint was throwing her off.

"I'm Mackenzie Ward. I run cross-country for Avondale. I'm a big fan."

Of me? Tessa was taken aback. She'd never met an actual fan before, let alone one who competed against her. "Oh. Um, thanks."

"Sorry to hear about your ankle. Everyone was so bummed but, like, seriously impressed."

With me falling in a ditch? "Well, Amelia was really helpful. She's great."

"Oh, yeah. Amelia is a sweetheart." Then, she shot a glance over her shoulder. "Just watch out for the newest member of your team." She mouthed, "Willow," and Tessa's curiosity was piqued.

Utilizing her well-honed interrogation techniques, Tessa decided to inquire further. "Not a fan of hers, huh?"

Mackenzie rolled her eyes and lowered her voice even more. "She's the worst teammate. I'll tell you, you can't trust her. Especially with guys. Just ask Amelia."

Tessa tried to hide her intrigue. "What exactly do you mean?"

"This guy Stephen on our team—really cute, really sweet. He was totally crushing on Amelia for, like, ever. Then,

Willow swoops in and goes after him. Wasn't even interested until she knew he liked her teammate."

"What happened?"

"Stephen chose Amelia. But Willow made them both miserable. We're still trying to get them back together."

A shiver moved up Tessa's spine, remembering how Willow elbowed Amelia right out of a race. Guilt started to surface for helping someone capable of that behavior. Then, studying Mackenzie, confusion entered her mind. "Um, not to be rude, but why are you at her party, then?"

Mackenzie shrugged. "Just keeping an eye on my friends who wanted to come. Like I said, I don't trust her."

Tessa wanted to keep the productive conversation going, but the tall blonde floated by her periphery again. "It was nice meeting you, Mackenzie. Hope to see you at track season."

"You bet, Tessa. Can't wait to watch you win a third championship!"

The short farewell was enough for Tessa to lose sight of the girl in the white dress. Pushing through one packed room after another, Tessa breathed a sigh of relief when she spotted the white dress again. As she squinted through the dim party lighting to examine the costume more closely, she noticed a pair of feathery wings on the back. Finally, when the girl turned, Tessa confirmed it was Willow—ironically dressed as an angel, down to the golden halo on her blonde head.

Tessa stepped forward mere inches before abruptly halting. Willow had cornered Mason and was flashing her most charming smile. As Mason nodded along, Willow placed a hand on his forearm and leaned in close. A sickness swirled in Tessa's gut. Was this all an attempt to get her boyfriend to Willow's party? Was this her plan all along? Maybe Tessa was the one being played.

Chapter 25

Why the long face, track star?"

Tessa was nearly blinded by a gleaming white suit, silver shirt, and gold tie, attached to a genuine smile and curly, dark hair. "Owen?" She gave him a once-over and almost couldn't believe her eyes. *A real costume!* "Or should I say Jay Gatsby?"

Owen proudly held his head up high as he adjusted his crisp collar. "I'm glad you noticed. I was trying to convince Nick to come as Gatsby's buddy of the same name, but he just wanted to wear his cross-country uniform. What kind of costume is that?"

One that ironically matches Riley's. They came as a couple after all—a running one.

Gesturing ahead, he said, "Looks like your Ned is getting cornered. Don't let the costume fool you. She's no angel."

Tessa's stomach lurched as the room seemed to spin. "I know. I've heard and seen."

"How about we go save him, Nancy? Perfect costume, by the way."

She nodded, glad to have backup.

"Hey, old sport," Owen shouted, slinging his arm around a surprised Mason.

"Wow. You look sharp," he said with a fist bump.

"Thanks. I was just chatting with your lovely Nancy here." He inserted himself between Mason and a speechless Willow.

Before Mason could say another word, Tessa produced her sweetest forced smile and grabbed Willow by the arm (incidentally, the same arm attached to the fingers previously touching Mason). "We'll be right back."

"What the heck, Tessa? Geez, you're strong for being four feet tall." Willow rubbed her arm as Tessa took her own opportunity to corner her.

"Four foot seven, actually. And it's called lifting. You should try it sometime."

Willow looked Tessa up and down, twisting her face into a grimace. "What on earth are you wearing? It's like a hundred years old."

"It's vintage. *Nancy Drew.* And you'd know that if you ever picked up a book. Try that too, sometime." She crossed her arms and shot Willow a stern look. "So, what's the plan?"

"Plan?" Willow was still rubbing her arm as her halo slipped farther down her head.

Ah, the irony, Tessa thought. "Yeah. You wanted my agency to help you. We're here. But I've yet to see any haunting, other than the lame, fake kind you manufactured for this party."

"Maybe you're not investigating hard enough or maybe you're not that great of a sleuth."

Tessa tried to rein in her anger, but it had reached visible limits. "Or maybe you're too preoccupied entertaining my boyfriend."

Willow grinned from ear to ear, clearly proud she'd struck a nerve. If this was her plan, Tessa had fallen for it—hook, line, and sinker. "Meet me upstairs in ten minutes. Outside the room with—"

"The round window—yeah, I know."

When Willow walked away, straightening her halo, Tessa let out a long exhale. *Why did I agree to this?*

"Everything okay?" Mason asked, snapping her back into the spooky present.

"Yeah. I just need to grab the girls."

Tessa turned away from him, and he gently pulled her back. "You don't want my help? I'm part of the team, right?" He smiled brightly, but Tessa couldn't bring herself to join him.

"You were ... I mean, you are. It's just ... I got everyone into this and need to get everyone out."

Mason appeared slightly wounded but nodded.

"Oh. Could you hold this for me? For safekeeping?" She offered Mason her cherished novel.

"Sure. And, before you go ..." He pulled her so close, she could see the detailed flecks in his eyes.

Tessa thought, *Maybe this is it.*

But he hesitated, then kissed her cheek. "Good luck."

Chapter 26

When Tessa ascended the tall, creaky flight up the old Victorian's second story, Skylar, Leah, and Riley were already congregating in the darkness with apprehensive looks. "This is mega creepy, Tessa," Leah said. "And it's not like I can make a fast getaway in this ginormous costume. I couldn't even get up those stairs without going sideways."

"At least you have a weapon," Skylar said, cocking her head toward Leah's huge paintbrush as she absently scratched some glitter off her cheek. "What am I supposed to do? Smother the ghost with a pompom?"

Riley's eyes magnified through her glasses. "I don't even have that. Can I borrow one?"

Tessa slapped her hand to her forehead. "No one is going to need a weapon."

"Oh, good. You're actually punctual," Willow said from the other end of the darkened hallway, making everyone but Tessa jump. "Especially considering *wide-load* and *limpy* over there," she said, pointing to Leah and Tessa.

"You wanna rethink those weapons?" Skylar whispered to Tessa, who nearly cracked a smile.

"Anyway, it's time we see this haunted room," Tessa announced to the group.

Willow sashayed across the hallway. "I thought you'd never ask." She paused in front of the closed door, then slowly opened it with a loud *creak* that echoed down the hall. The girls hesitated until Willow waved them in with annoyance. "Well?"

When no one stepped forward, Tessa sighed and walked into the pitch-black room. "Lights?" she asked.

"This is all I have," Willow said, flipping on one single lamp. It illuminated a canopy bed and a tall antique dresser, which flanked the door on one wall.

As she moved farther inside, Tessa felt herself involuntarily shiver and she hugged her arms to her chest. "Is there heat in here?"

"Yeah. But it's temperamental. My parents are getting it fixed."

With her business face on, Tessa took a stroll around the spacious room while her friends slowly inched their way inside. She had to admit, there was an air of creepiness to the room that would certainly give her pause to make this her permanent sleeping chamber. Along the exterior walls were several square windows and one round one. Dark blue wallpaper with a faded floral design covered the walls from floor to ceiling. As Tessa toured the edges of the room, the old wooden floor planks squeaked at her feet. She stuck her head inside a closet, brimming with Willow's clothes and some stray moving boxes. When she noticed the box labeled "Willow's Books" left unopened in a corner, she snickered to herself. Finally, she made her way to a large bookcase, which ironically could have housed those books.

"Okay," she said, whirling around. "Where has all this haunting taken place?"

Willow stepped forward, clearly irritated that Tessa hadn't already solved this in two quick minutes. "I showed you the curtains. And it's cold all the time. Oh, and I hear sounds late at night."

Tessa was trying to take this seriously, but these seemed like average "I live in an old house" scenarios.

"What kind of sounds?" Leah asked, stepping forward to join Tessa.

"Like a girl or moaning," Willow said.

"Which is it?" Tessa asked. Willow's face flashed impatience. "Was it a girl or moaning?"

Willow threw up her hands. "I don't know. Aren't you the experts?"

"Not at this," Skylar said, and Willow shot her a stink eye.

"Well, I haven't seen anything here out of the ordinary, even for Halloween," Tessa said. "You mentioned we'd have access to the whole house. What other rooms might be helpful?"

Pondering this for a few beats, Willow said, "I guess the attic might help. All sorts of old stuff was left here."

"Okay. Let's try that."

But Willow remained stationary. "Only problem. There isn't any light up there."

"You have got to be kidding me," Leah said.

"I'm out," Skylar said, throwing up her pompom-filled hands and heading for the hallway. "I've got better things to do."

Willow sneered. "Yeah. Like follow Ethan around like a lost puppy. How pathetic."

"What did you just say?" Skylar's eyes glowed from more than just glitter.

"You heard me."

Leah jumped in, using her palette as a defensive wall and separating Skylar from lunging at Willow. "We're gonna go. Clearly, this is a job for way less people."

Tessa nodded, indicating she had it covered as the two girls disappeared. "Do you have a flashlight?" she asked Willow.

When Willow went off to get some lights, Tessa turned to a trembling Riley. "Can you stay here and watch the room?"

"By … myself?"

Taking her by the shoulders, Tessa said, "There's nothing to be afraid of, Riley. And we won't be far."

Riley's expression turned into panic. "Shoot! I gave my cell phone to Nick because my pockets are too small. What if I need to call for help?"

Tessa blew out a long exhale. "Here. Take mine," she said, shoving her phone into her best friend's palm. "Just stand in the hallway, by the door. Let us know if anything weird happens."

"What's weird?" she asked as Tessa went to follow Willow.

"I don't know. A ghost?"

Tessa left Riley looking freaked out and met Willow at the foot of another staircase, leading to the ink-black eaves of the roof. "It's up there," she said, handing her a flashlight.

When Willow didn't move, Tessa sighed, clicked on the torch, and carefully mounted the rickety wooden staircase. "I take it you're coming," she called back through the stairs' creaking, and Willow reluctantly followed.

Shining the thin stream of yellow light up the staircase, Tessa felt a surge of adrenaline. This was exactly what sleuthing was all about. They reached the top in quick order and ended up in a vast space encircled by old wooden beams and uneven flooring. Antique items were scattered around the perimeter with a large bookcase along a side wall. As

Tessa stepped farther into the room, goosebumps formed on her arms from the familiar chill that she'd experienced in Willow's bedroom.

"Yuck. This place is gross," Willow said, tiptoeing around the dusty, cobwebbed artifacts.

"You should have had the party up here," Tessa said. "No decorating involved."

As Tessa made her way around the room, she was drawn to a large, round painting in an ornate gold frame, unhung and leaning against the far wall. When she got closer, Willow gasped. "That's her."

"Her?"

"Yeah. The girl in the window. I swear I've seen her."

Bending at her waist, Tessa inspected the painting. A girl with long, red hair stared back at her with a vacant expression. While dressed in a flowy white gown, the girl's ghostly image was best described as "creepy." *She does look familiar,* Tessa thought. Then again, maybe it was just the legend entering her subconscious.

Leaving the painting, Tessa headed to the bookcase with eagerness. This one was actually filled with old hardcovers. "Wow. It's a whole library."

Willow grimaced, keeping her distance. "Are you almost done?"

Ignoring her, Tessa poised her finger on the spines and skimmed the titles, including classics, poetry, even history. "This is an incredible collection."

"That's right. You're a bookworm," Willow said with a yawn, clearly not impressed.

As Tessa reached for a book, her foot slipped on an uneven plank of flooring, pushing her against the bookcase. "Shoot!" she said, hitting a shelf with her hip. Suddenly, the bookcase turned, revealing an entrance to another stair-case, going downward. "No way! A real secret passageway!"

Willow almost appeared interested until an eerie *moan* from below echoed around them. "There it is again. I told you."

"What the heck is that?" Tessa asked, leaning into the darkened passageway. As she stepped down with her good foot, the top step caved in. "Argh!" she shouted, falling a few steps below. Thankfully, she still held on to the flash-light. "Willow?" she called out, trying to catch her breath. *I really need to stay off my feet for the rest of the year.* Sitting up on the steps, she glanced back at the top of the stair-case. "Willow? Can you help?" But there was no answer and no light above. All of a sudden, it was clear to Tessa that she was alone. And the moaning continued.

Chapter 27

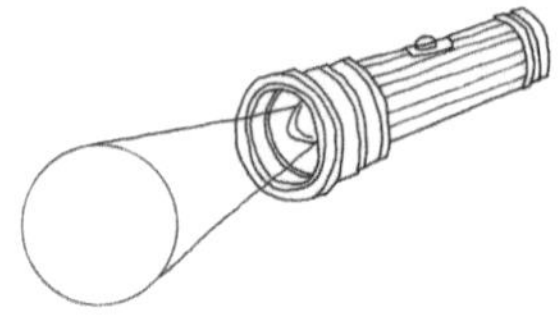

Fear enveloped Tessa. She was stuck in the middle of a staircase to who knows where, hoping her ankle was okay, with only one flashlight to guide her. And she was alone, completely alone in the cocoon-like passageway. Tessa could cry out, but to whom? Now that the moaning had ceased, it was replaced with the muffled *thumps* of dance music downstairs. She instinctively reached for her cell phone, then groaned, "I gave it to Riley!"

Stay calm, the young sleuth told herself. With the top step missing, the only easy way out was down. "In the dark," she said. Standing, Tessa clicked on the flashlight and concentrated it below. She moved down a step and was thankful her ankle seemed unharmed. But only one more step down and her torch dimmed. "Thanks for the bad batteries, Willow."

She was about to attempt another step when she heard a muted, "Tessa?" from above with a flash of light.

"Hello?" she said, a slight quivering in her voice. When she faced the top of the staircase, her heart skipped a beat, then relaxed. "Mason?"

A set of emerald eyes came into focus in the dimmed light of her torch. "Are you okay?"

"Yeah. The top step caved in. Is Willow there?"

Mason kneeled into the staircase, shining his flashlight on her. "No. I got worried and went to find you. Riley pointed to where you went, and I found this on the floor near the doorway."

"At least Willow is consistent." *Consistently useless.*

"What can I do?"

Tessa was torn. Have Mason help her go back the way she came? Or let her curiosity get the better of her and follow the passageway? "I'm gonna keep going. Can I, um, use your flashlight?"

Mason considered this for a split second. "Sure." And then, he leapt over the bad step and was by her side in a jiffy.

"What are you doing?"

He handed her his flashlight and took her dimmed one. "Tessa, you don't really think I'm letting you do this on your own?"

"Mason, I don't need rescuing. All the time anyway," she mumbled the last part.

"Oh, I'm not rescuing. I'm backup."

Tessa's new light also started to dim. "Argh. I'm gonna kill Willow."

"We'd better get going, then."

Heaving a heavy sigh, Tessa waved him down. They made it a couple more steps into near darkness when they heard another *moan.* "It does sound like a girl." Mason raised an eyebrow. "Just something Willow said." As she stood in the faint glow of their flashlights, Tessa had to admit she felt safer with Mason there. She reached for his hand before continuing down the final steps until they literally hit a wall. "I guess we're gonna find out where this goes."

She started to reach forward as a piercing scream cut through the silence. Tessa and Mason were pushing through the opening when they heard another scream mere feet away. When they stepped through the doorway, Tessa's mouth dropped to the floor. "Seriously? We're in the same room."

Mason looked confused again. "The same room?"

"Yeah. Willow's bedroom. This is her bookcase."

The room was now dark. Tessa waved her flashlight across the space until it landed on a long, white dress leaving the room. "Was that Willow?" Mason asked.

"I don't think so. I didn't see any wings."

Suddenly, the room was illuminated, where Riley was standing by the lamp near the bed. "Oh, thank goodness it's you guys."

"Riley, was that you screaming?"

"The first one. I thought I saw something. Willow screamed after and ran off."

Tessa scratched her head. "None of this makes any sense."

"Wait. Did you guys come through there?" Riley asked. She pointed to the bookcase, then turned slightly pale.

"Yeah. Why?"

"That's where I saw someone. Before you came down."

Without another word, Tessa sprinted to the hallway as fast as her ankle would allow her. Willow was nowhere to be found—again. But the attic door was still ajar. "Riley, was this left open after Mason came up?"

"Nope."

"Yeah. I closed it on my way up," he said.

"Tessa, is this the ghost?" Riley asked.

She shook her head. "More like a prankster. I'm sure of it. You guys stay here. I'm going back to the bedroom."

When Tessa arrived back inside the "haunted bedroom," sure enough, the bookcase door was moving. "Stop!" she shouted and reached forward. Her hand caught some white fabric, and she was face-to-face with a red head of hair. "Amelia?!"

She held her finger over her lips and waved Tessa up the staircase. When they were halfway up, Amelia spun around with her flashlight. If Tessa didn't know any better, this dimmed view of the tiny runner was a spitting image of the painting in the attic. "Please don't tell," she whispered.

"But how?"

"All of us from Avondale used to come by here when it was a vacant house. Snuck inside and learned all the ins and outs. Even the passageways."

"And when you found out Willow was moving here, you decided to get back at her. For Stephen, right?"

Amelia nodded as her face fell. "She was so mean to us. I just wanted to scare her a little. Put her in her place."

Tessa couldn't contain the smile that spilled across her face. "It was a pretty great plan, honestly."

Amelia's smile returned. "Thanks."

"But how did you get down there with me at the top of these stairs?"

"I was waiting at the bottom, until you guys left the room for the attic. After all this time, I've gotten pretty good at haunting."

Tessa hooked an arm around her. "Oh, Amelia. You are seriously my hero—twice over."

They chuckled, and then Amelia asked, "What's the plan now?"

"Let's see," Tessa said, tapping her finger to her chin. "I think it can't hurt for Willow to get haunted a tad more. It is Halloween, after all."

Chapter 28

"Wait. So, Amelia? Really?" Leah said, her eyes showing disbelief as Tessa gave the girls a play-by-play of her adventures in the attic as they huddled around the refreshment table.

Grabbing a cookie resembling a ghost, Skylar looked so delighted, she was practically giddy. "This is the best Halloween ever. And remind me to buy Amelia a gift."

Riley let out a held breath. "But what are we going to do about …?"

Just then, Willow stormed into the room, her face as pale as her dress. "I'll take care of it," Tessa grumbled. "Catch up with you guys later."

With the girls jetting off in different directions, Tessa sucked in an exasperated breath. She'd already spent way more time with Willow than she'd bargained for. Now, she wanted to enjoy an evening of food, music, and socially acceptable dress-up. "Well, are you going to do something or not?" Willow asked, crossing her arms.

Tessa shrugged. "What is there to do? I didn't find any-thing." She fiercely bit her lip, trying to suppress a smile. *This is kind of fun.*

The color returned to Willow's face with a vengeance. "Are you serious? You heard the moaning. You investigated the passageway."

Selecting a cookie in the shape of a pumpkin, dusted with orange sanding sugar, Tessa said, "Yes. The passage-way where you *left* me, in the dark, by the way. But, again, I didn't find anything. So, as far as the TSLR Agency is con-cerned—case closed."

With a huff, Willow spun around, her wings taking flight. "I knew you'd be useless. Good riddance."

Tessa stood there, grinning and nibbling on her cookie when she spotted Amelia heading for the door. But, before she and her Avondale friends left, she gave Tessa a wink—both girls' jobs done for the evening.

"I believe this is yours, super sleuth," Mason said, hand-ing Tessa her book. "Owen was good enough to keep it safe while we finished our investigating."

Tessa cradled the book affectionately. "Thank you. And, um, thanks for the backup earlier."

"So, what are your plans for the rest of the evening?" He leaned in with his eyes twinkling under the faint glow of the chandelier.

Reaching for his hands, she said, "Since the sleuthing is done, it's about time we appreciated this blaring music."

They moved to the middle of the large living room, where a space in front of an old fireplace was reserved as a dance floor. As they spun around ghosts, witches, uniformed ath-letes, and shimmery capes, Tessa noticed Riley, enjoying an intimate chat with Nick. When Tessa waved to her, Riley also pulled Nick onto the dance floor with a giggle. But the most entertaining part of the evening was watching Skylar and Leah having a blast while ignoring Ethan and Caleb, who sulked in the corner with their *championship* attire.

When the girls had danced themselves into exhaustion and Skylar was no longer sparkling with head-to-toe glitter, they decided to call it a night. "Let's take a selfie outside before we leave, to remember Halloween at Huntington Manor," Leah suggested.

"Yeah. I definitely won't forget this haunted house," Skylar said with a chuckle.

Corralling everyone, the group ventured outside, past the fake graveyard, where the vampire had long disappeared, perhaps enjoying a night's slumber in his coffin. They lined up underneath the eerie halo of a full moon while Mason snapped photos of the girls in front of the legendary haunted Huntington Manor.

"Ooh, let's see," Riley said, reaching for the cell phone and swiping the screen to view the photos.

The girls giggled, pointing to their fun poses and faces. Then, suddenly they got quiet as they spun around in unison, staring at the round window in the middle of the old Victorian. But there was nothing there.

Skylar grabbed the phone from Riley. "Tessa, do you see that?"

She slowly nodded, feeling herself shudder.

"But how?" Leah asked, rubbing her eyes.

"Maybe it's still Amelia," Riley suggested.

But Tessa shook her head. "I saw her leave earlier. No way she came back."

"What is it?" Mason asked as a *hush* fell over the girls.

Without a word, Tessa pointed to the photo he had just taken. Under the radiance of the full moon, Huntington Manor certainly looked spooky. But it wasn't the fake graveyard or the dilapidated exterior that enhanced the mood. It was the blurry image of a girl, standing in the round window, *her red hair framed by the delicate arch.*

"So, it's true," Skylar said softly.

No one else spoke, but they were all thinking the same thing. *Regardless of Amelia or even the TSLR Detective Agency, the haunting of Huntington Manor would continue.*

Chapter 29

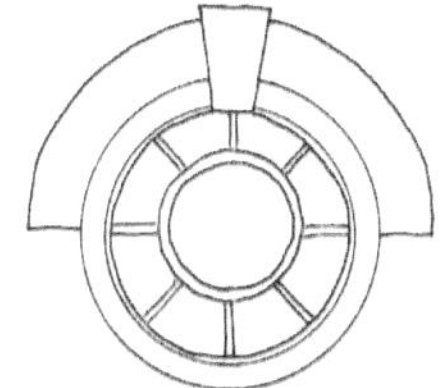

As Tessa awoke the next morning to the autumn sun pouring through her windows, she was still scratching her head over the previous night's events. Her heart pounded as she recalled the exciting attic passageway discovery that led to Amelia's brilliant haunting plan. If only that were the most curious aspect of the night. Tessa shook her head to clear the cobwebs and grabbed her cell phone from the nightstand. She swiped to the photo of her friends outside the manor and her breath caught at the blurred image framed by the arched window. "Well, it wasn't a dream." But it was perplexing.

Throwing off the covers, she heaved herself out of her massive sleigh bed. Tessa skimmed the room, which looked as scattered as her thoughts. After an exhausting evening, she'd randomly tossed her lovely blue knit dress on the floor beside her closet. Her Keds were thrown on different sides of the room. *How did that even happen?* But thankfully, her antique *Nancy Drew* book was carefully sitting on her desk.

She gingerly stepped on her right foot, grinning when it didn't bother her at all. "Track season, here we come," she said to herself.

In fact, Tessa was in such a good mood, she scooped up her shoes and, with some humming, started cleaning the room. She was arranging the throw pillows meticulously on her bed when there was a soft knock on the door. "Come in."

Tessa's mom peeked her head inside. "Oh, good. You're awake, sweetie. Don't forget about the induction ceremony today."

"Uh … right," Tessa said, squirming as she scrunched up her face. Forgetting the induction ceremony was *precisely* what she'd done. "Um, what do I wear?" Her eyes instantly slid to the mess remaining on the floor.

"Just a skirt or something like that. Nothing too fancy."

Tapping her bottom lip, Tessa stared at her closet for a few beats.

When she noticed her daughter's hesitation, Dr. Wright walked in and headed to the racks of clothes. "You have lots of nice things to choose from here."

"Is Dad excited?" Tessa asked, flopping onto her freshly made bed.

Her mom stuck her head out from the depths of the hanging clothes. "I think so. A bit anxious too. He's been avoiding this for a while."

Tessa nodded, knowing this was true. After much discussion and near-begging on the part of the community, Mayor Greene, and outgoing Chief Woodbridge, Detective Wright had finally agreed to accept the position as the new Chief of Police for Greeneville Heights. The deal was sealed after Dan Dunbar and his accomplices were charged with a slew of crimes, including the business break-ins around downtown.

"How about this?" Tessa's mom held up a green and navy-blue plaid skirt with a matching blue sweater. "It will bring out your eyes."

Tessa took the outfit and hung it up in her bathroom. "Mom, can I ditch the ankle bandage, though? It's gonna be awkward with tights."

"Sure. Fine," she said with a sigh. Then, she blew out another sigh at Tessa's room. "This is going to require some elbow grease."

"Sorry," Tessa said sheepishly. "You told me to stay off my ankle."

Dr. Wright started picking up the piles of clothes, shoes, and books. "I'll take care of this. You focus on getting ready."

Twenty minutes later, Tessa slipped on her navy flats, excited for her dad's special day. "Wow," she said, taking a visual tour of the spotless room. "Thanks, Mom."

"You're welcome, and you look lovely," she said, hanging up Tessa's 1940s costume dress. "They really knew how to dress way back when. This is so stylish." She was reaching into the vintage front pockets, when she furrowed her brows. "What the …?"

"What, Mom?"

Dr. Wright pulled out what appeared to be a gold bracelet and held it up to the light. "This is beautiful."

"Is that a … charm bracelet?" Tessa asked, pointing to several little gold objects dangling from the chain.

"Looks like it. And a nice one too." Then, she searched the dress from top to bottom. "Was this inside when we got it at Cleo's?"

Tessa reached inside the pocket and inspected its details. "It must have been. Look, the pocket has layers of fabric. I bet it was stuck between one of them. Should we tell Cleo?"

"We can. But knowing Cleo, she'll agree with the legal and world view of *finders, keepers*." Tessa's mom dropped the stunning bracelet into her daughter's palm.

"Really? I wonder where it came from. I bet there's an exciting story." Tessa felt her pulse racing. She was certain there was more to this bracelet than a simple tucked-away token.

Dr. Wright pushed some of Tessa's bob behind her ear. "Something tells me if anyone can get to the bottom of it, you can, sweetie. In the meantime, we are due downtown in less than an hour."

Absently nodding as her mom rushed out of her bedroom, Tessa continued to stare at the bracelet, shimmering in the morning light. She was about to place it back inside the dress pocket, then couldn't help herself. Tessa slipped it over her tiny wrist. "*Finders, keepers*, huh?"

Chapter 30

Minutes later, Tessa bounded down the staircase and into the kitchen, but skidded to a stop when she saw her dad standing by the marble island. He was sipping a mug of coffee while studying some notecards marked up with his handwriting. But it was his appearance that floored Tessa, and she had to stop herself from saying "Wow" out loud. His salt-and-mostly-peppered hair was freshly trimmed, and he was wearing a pressed police dress uniform in dark blue. Beside him on the island sat his matching peaked cap. The whole scene made Tessa proud beyond words.

When Detective Wright shifted his gaze from his cards to his daughter, his lips curved into a smile. "Morning, sweetie."

Tessa ran to her dad and wrapped her arms around his formal jacket. "Congratulations, Dad. You look amazing."

"Thank you," he said softly, squeezing her. "You look pretty amazing yourself."

"Are you nervous about your speech?"

"A little," he said, kissing the top of her head. "I just want to do the town and my family proud."

Tessa stared up at her dad and into his sapphire eyes. "Dad, there's no question that's gonna happen."

His smile widened. "Well, a lot of this is thanks to you, helping me with cases. You wanna be my assistant? We can swear you in today too?"

She chuckled at her dad's joke. "Nah. I'll stick with my hugely successful detective agency. I think I'm already on the cusp of a new case."

Detective Wright lifted an eyebrow along with his coffee mug. "New case, huh? This isn't dangerous, is it?"

Pouring herself a glass of orange juice, Tessa shook her head. "It's more of a found item situation."

"Intriguing," he said, his expression sincere.

Then, Tessa's mom floated into the kitchen in a classy mid-century modern sheath dress in light blue with nude kitten heels. "Oh, wow, Mom. That's the one you got at Cleo's, right?"

The coffee mug nearly slipped out of Tessa's dad's fingers. "Um, wow is right, Cora."

Dr. Wright's cheeks glowed a rosy red. "I know it's probably too much, but I couldn't resist after seeing your dress," she said to Tessa.

"Wow," Detective Wright repeated. "Very Jackie O." He forgot about his notecards on the island and gave his wife a kiss.

Rolling her eyes, Tessa said, "So, are we ready?"

"Almost," her mom said. "Hanna is getting Cam changed and dressed. She was nice enough to come with us today."

Tessa's dad hugged both his wife and daughter into his broad chest. "With my favorite ladies by my side, this day will be perfect."

* * *

To say that downtown Greeneville Heights was filled with pomp and circumstance was an understatement, especially considering an actual band was performing on a stage. Tessa's dad heaved a heavy sigh as they drove by while searching for parking around the packed police station property. A uniformed officer waved their SUV to a front spot, then saluted. "This is gonna be a long day," Detective Wright mumbled, his previous smile replaced with a creased forehead. Tessa knew he had requested a "simple affair" with his family by his side. This was far from it.

Tessa stared at Cam facing her in his car seat, taking a nap. *Sure. Now, you're quiet. You'd better not scream your head off in a little while.*

After they'd parked, Tessa's dad rushed off to prepare for the ceremony, and Hanna arrived in her car separately to roll Cam around. Dr. Wright took Tessa's hand. Based upon its trembling, she knew it was more for her mom than her. "How's your ankle, sweetie?" she asked absentmindedly as her eyes darted around the crowd.

"It's fine, Mom. Everything's going to be fine."

Tessa and her mom were ushered to a seating area on the platform stage behind the podium. All around them, people with elated expressions were shaking hands. It seemed that most of the town had congregated on this beautiful late-autumn day. Squinting up at the sun-drenched sky, Tessa got goosebumps, sensing the importance of the occasion.

Then, she spotted Mayor Lauren Greene ascending the stage steps with her husband, shaking hands along the way. Mason followed closely behind with his brother, Alex, who Tessa almost didn't recognize. Both sons were wearing suits, especially unusual for drummer Alex. But Tessa's gaze was focused on Mason. She'd seen him in a suit before when he'd taken her to last spring's school dance. All of a sudden, she felt especially warm in her sweater, even with the cool fall breeze.

Mason's emerald eyes, perfectly matching his tie, were on Tessa, and he waved coyly as they approached. "Congratulations, Cora," Mayor Greene said to Tessa's mom, giving her a genuine hug. She did the same for Tessa. "You and your mom look lovely," she added.

Walking with purpose to the podium, Mayor Greene clearly wanted to get this thing started. As Mason and his family took their seats a few chairs away, he sent Tessa a wink.

The next several minutes were filled with boisterous applause, ceremonial tasks, and Tessa's mom sneaking apprehensive glances at Cam's stroller. Thankfully, her brother was still sleeping peacefully, surely the result of Hanna's gentle rocking.

Even without looking at the podium, Tessa knew her dad had been introduced because the cheers could be heard for miles. Sliding a glance at her trembling mom, she took her hand and squeezed it.

Detective Wright's speech had both a distinguished and moving feel to it—very much how he approached being a retired Marine and police officer. Tessa's mom held back tears, and even Hanna appeared proud. When her dad was ready to be sworn in, Tessa and her mom stood beside him, Mayor Greene, and outgoing Chief Woodbridge.

During his oath, Detective Wright was emotional yet steady (his voice and uplifted palm unwavering), the sight making Tessa's heart swell. And when she stared out into the crowd at all her friends and neighbors (many who were like family), she understood why her dad was doing this, even if he was somewhat wary about it.

"Ladies and gentlemen of Greeneville Heights," Mayor Greene proclaimed. "I am so very honored to announce for the first time, our new Police Chief, Drew Wright. Thank you, Chief Wright, for everything you've done for our town and will continue to do."

The applause was deafening as the entire stage sprang to its feet. Tessa's and Mason's eyes met, and he gave her a thumbs-up. The best part was that Tessa's dad, now Chief Wright, was beaming—all and all, a pretty perfect day.

Chapter 31

After the ceremony, the Wrights were bombarded by well-wishers. Waving to her mom, Tessa managed to escape through the chaos in time to run smack-dab into Mason. "Hey, Tessa." He leaned in for a quick hug, and they headed down the platform and away from the crowd. "Your dad was great up there."

"Thanks," Tessa said, grinning from ear to ear at her dad. "I think he was worried about his speech but nailed it as usual."

Mason gave her a once over. "You look awesome, by the way. Done with the ankle bandage, huh?"

"Oh, thanks," she said, fidgeting with her skirt. "Yeah, my mom was feeling extra generous today. She still wants me to wear a brace for running, though." She pointed to his formal attire. "I like your suit. Very handsome."

Holding his chin high, he lifted his tie and smoothed it out. "I am proud to say my mom picked this out all by herself. Something about my 'eyes.'" He used air quotes and shook his head.

Tessa giggled. "Moms are like that. And she was right." When the wind kicked up, she raised her hand to push some unruly hair off her face.

"Is that new?" Mason pointed to her wrist and the charm bracelet, glistening in the sun.

"Oh. Um. Kind of." She leaned in to whisper. "I sort of *found* it … in my dress from Cleo's."

Mason's eyes widened. "Really? That's a lucky find. It's very Tessa."

She fiddled with the bracelet on her wrist. "I wish I could figure out where it came from. I bet it's a great story."

Bending close, he inspected the bracelet. "It reminds me of your necklace." He gently touched Tessa's necklace that she was gifted for her last birthday. It was also gold with a dangling charm of a winged shoe. Tessa's parents said it reminded them of her flying down the track at her meets.

Tessa's jaw fell to the ground. "You're right. The charms are similar. My parents got my necklace at Carmichael's. I wonder if Ellie or Gene would recognize this bracelet."

"Well, I thought I saw Ellie, at least, before the ceremony started." Eileen and Gene Carmichael were the elderly owners of Greeneville Heights' most respected jeweler. Their store had been around for several generations.

Grabbing Mason by the arm, Tessa steered them through the crowd. "Where? Which row?"

Mason chuckled. "The first row."

Tessa squinted through the familiar faces of Greeneville, hoping to find just the right one. "Eureka!" she exclaimed when she'd located Eileen Carmichael, chatting with Bobby Warren and his fiancée Aimee. *I bet he's trying to get a good deal on wedding bands.*

"Hey, runnah!" Bobby shouted before Tessa had a chance to say a greeting.

Eileen, always the pinnacle of proper decorum, cordially offered her hand. "Wonderful to see you again, Tessa. You must be so proud of your father."

"Oh, thanks. Yes."

"Your mom did a great job too," Bobby said to Mason. "You remember Aimee, the love of my life," he teased while dramatically clutching his chest.

The pretty brunette playfully smacked Bobby's arm. "Just ignore him. His job for the rest of our lives is to drive me nuts."

Tessa couldn't help but laugh. Bobby and Aimee were perfect for each other—perfectly goofy. "We actually had a question for you, Ellie."

Aimee started pulling Bobby away. "That's our cue. We'll give you guys some peace and quiet," she teased. Then, she whispered to Tessa, shooting a glance at Mason. "Very cute guy you have there. He's a keeper."

Heat crept up Tessa's cheeks, hoping Mason didn't hear Aimee's unusually loud voice, but she gave a definitive nod.

"What did you want to ask, dear?" Eileen asked as her gaze fell on Tessa's necklace. "Oh, I remember when your parents came in to purchase this. 'A perfect gift for the perfect runner,' they said."

Mason nudged Tessa, and her face was burning as she ran her fingers over her necklace. "Yeah. It was an amazing gift." Then, she held up her wrist. "I was wondering if you recognized this. The charms are the same style."

Eileen slipped on her reading glasses and inspected the bracelet. Immediately, her eyes brightened. "Oh, yes. It is most certainly from our store. Right here." She carefully handled Tessa's running shoe charm, then compared it to one on the bracelet. "We always engrave a tiny 'C' on all our jewelry. For Carmichael's."

Tessa gasped. Sure enough, her necklace charm and the bracelet ones were each engraved with a tiny letter **C**. "Do you remember this bracelet?"

Chuckling, Eileen shook her curly white head of hair. "No. Unfortunately not. We've been making charms and bracelets for decades. But it does appear rather on the older side."

Tessa's heart sank. *There goes my lead.*

"Where did you get it, my dear? Was it passed down?"

She shot a glance at Mason and swallowed hard. "Um, no. Kind of a lucky find."

"This beauty certainly is lucky, that's for sure. It's what we always say to our customers when they buy charms from us. We hope they are good luck to all who enjoy them." Seeing Tessa's disappointment, Eileen said, "You know, Gene is the one who makes all the charms. He's busy at the store today and had to miss the ceremony. Why don't you stop by and have him give it a look? He may remember such an exquisite specimen."

"Oh, yes. That sounds great," Tessa said, her face lighting up.

Eileen patted her on the back. "We'll look forward to seeing you."

As Tessa held back her giddiness, Mason regarded her for a moment. "You have that Tessa look again," he said with a smirk, yanking her out of her thoughts.

"What do you mean?" she asked innocently.

"You know, that look you get when you're on the cusp of a new case."

Tessa held her head up high. "Does that mean you're not interested in my next sleuthing adventure?"

"Oh, no. I'm very interested," he said, threading his fingers through hers. "I'm your backup, remember?"

"So, we're in this together, then?"

"Anything to help Greeneville's best super sleuth."

Chapter 32

It was a perfect night for a meteor shower with a clear autumn sky, and everyone in Greeneville Heights seemed to have ventured out for the show. Tessa and Riley walked down busy Main Street ahead of Tessa's parents, pushing Cam's stroller as it crunched the spent leaves on the sidewalk. Sue Ann joined them, having just closed up her salon for the evening.

"Aren't you excited?" Tessa asked Riley, elbowing her. While everyone camped out at the park for the best seats, the plan was for Tessa and Riley to split off to meet up with Mason and Nick. Of course, that would give Riley the opportunity to hang out with her date on her own.

"I don't know. What if he thinks this is a 'friends' thing?"

Tessa hooked her arm around her best friend. "Then, you at least know where he stands, right? You'll still have a great time hanging out together. You always do."

That seemed to perk her up. "True. And I'm totally going to join the Amateur Astronomy Society tonight. They're even setting up telescopes in the park to view the moon and some constellations up close."

Peering over her shoulder, Tessa was pleased to see her parents relaxed and holding hands as they strolled past colorful street trees and glowing streetlamps. It kind of reminded her of walking this same route with Mason, and a light giddiness stirred in her gut. Even Cam seemed in awe of the evening, captivated by Sue Ann's constant chatter in her southern twang as her curly red hair bobbed up and down. There was something about the cool, crisp air that gave Tessa a feeling that tonight was going to be special.

At the entrance to the park, Tessa gestured to her parents that she and Riley were going off on their own. "Curfew," Dr. Wright mouthed, and Tessa gave her a thumbs-up understanding.

Riley fidgeted, then glanced at her watch. "Shoot. I only have a little over an hour before my mom wants me home." It was well-known that Riley's curfew time was much earlier than everyone else's.

"Don't stress," Tessa advised. "Relax and have fun. The shower will start soon anyway." Then, she spotted Nick approaching. "Okay. You're on. I'm going to meet Mason."

Nodding repeatedly, Riley was clearly trying to psych herself up. But she was failing miserably. In fact, Tessa was worried she was going to throw up any second. "Uh, you sure you got this?"

"Yup. Totally. Where are you meeting Mason?" she asked, her eyes still on Nick in the distance.

"He said to text him when I'm here, and he'll give me directions. Very cryptic."

Before Riley could chicken out again, Tessa bolted into the park and quickly texted Mason about her arrival. He immediately sent a text back. It was a list of lefts and rights all around the park and Greeneville's lake.

As Tessa worked her way through the directions, she started to wonder if he was leading her on some wild goose chase or a little adventure. Not only was she taking an extended tour of the spacious park, but she had to weave around group after group huddled together with their chins up to the sky, ready for the main event.

Tessa was about to give up and find her parents (who she astonishingly had yet to run into) when she received one final text:

Maple tree, straight ahead.

And sure enough, there was Mason Greene, relaxing against the trunk of a majestic maple. It was strikingly similar to the one in her own backyard which housed her treehouse.

He waved, and her heart skipped around a little. As Tessa approached, she noticed him carrying a large stadium blanket and two paper cups. "I thought you were going to stand me up," she joked.

"Well, I *am* still standing," he joked back, elbowing the tree trunk behind him. "And, sorry about all the walking. Is your ankle okay?"

"Yup. It was good to get some exercise. What's this?" She pointed to the cups.

"Oh. Here," he said, offering her one. "Caramel apple cider from Lorraine's. It's as awesome as it sounds."

"I bet." She took a sip and enjoyed hot, sweet, and creamy apple goodness. "Yum. That is seriously an autumn apple orchard in a cup."

Mason laughed and pushed off the maple's trunk. He placed his cup on the ground and spread out the blanket on the lush, green grass. Tessa once again noticed his evergreen sweatshirt, then wished she'd bundled up more herself as a cool breeze cut across the shimmering lake. "Maybe I should have brought another blanket," he said, seeing her shiver.

"Oh, I'm fine. How did you find this spot? The whole park is packed except here." They settled onto the blanket and sipped their ciders.

"That's a little secret. My mom used to take Alex and me here when we were kids. People tend to hang out on the other side of the lake because it's easier to get to."

As the tree's hefty limbs swayed above them, Tessa tilted her head back to view the clear, black sky dotted with twinkling stars. "It really is a great view. The shower is gonna be awesome." Then, she turned to face Mason. "Are you gonna make a wish?"

He raised one eyebrow. "A wish?"

"Yeah. You always have to make a wish on a shooting star. And tonight is gonna be full of them. Lots of chances for one to come true."

Mason smiled sheepishly. "Well, I've never seen a shooting star before, so I'm a newbie about the rules." He playfully nudged Tessa and she giggled.

As another breeze swept by, rustling the colorful leaves above them, Tessa shivered again and gripped her track jacket tightly to her torso. "You're cold," Mason said, starting to remove his sweatshirt.

"What are you doing?"

"I'm giving you my sweatshirt, so you don't freeze."

But Tessa waved it off. "Mason, I'm fine. You shouldn't freeze because I didn't dress warm enough."

Sighing, Mason slipped his sweatshirt back on. "So, do you know what you're going to wish for?"

"Yup," she said, trying to keep her teeth from chattering. She hugged her knees to her chest in a desperate attempt to stop more goosebumps from forming.

Out of the blue, Mason wrapped his arms around her. Caught off guard, Tessa shivered, this time, solely due to their proximity. "If you won't let me give you my sweatshirt, my sweatshirt will come to you."

Tessa giggled, now bundled up in Mason's cozy warmth. "Thanks!" As they snuggled close, she hoped he couldn't hear her pounding heart or the butterflies stirring wildly in her stomach.

He glanced upward. "It's almost time. You ready to make your wish?" His voice was a soft whisper as his breath warmed her cheek.

Before she could answer, a glowing star streaked across the sky like a sparkler. "Did you see it?" she shouted, pointing above them in excitement. More stars twinkled in the dark sky, creating their own light show. Tessa shut her eyes tight and made her wish.

Mason was quiet throughout, cuddling her. When she turned to face him, his eyes appeared serious. As they locked with Tessa's, she felt herself tremble, but not from the cold. Then, Mason gently leaned toward her, pressing his lips to hers. *A real kiss!* It was as sweet and warm as the caramel apple cider. Tessa didn't even realize she had been holding her breath until he slowly pulled away.

A comfortable silence enveloped them as Mason hugged her into his sweatshirt while stars continued to streak and flash across the sky. It really was a special night. After a few more seconds, he whispered into her ear, "Do you think your wish will come true?"

Yes, Mason Greene. It already has.

Author's Note

So, I finally did it! I put Tessa on a hidden staircase aglow with a flashlight. It took three books, but there is no way I could have a *Nancy Drew*-inspired series without this nostalgic scene coming up eventually.

AUTUMN & HALLOWEEN INSPIRATION

As a writer, I tend to revolve my plots around the seasons. This creates atmospheric detail that stimulates the five senses and draws the reader into the story. In the previous two books in *The Wright Detective* series, the southern town of Greeneville Heights is always described in terms of its insufferable heat and blazing sun. So, adding cool fall breezes, colorful foliage, and cozy warm beverages was quite a departure. However, there is nothing like the beauty and comfort of the fall months. Also, the change in seasons provides me the opportunity to show growth and change in the town and the characters. While Tessa describes Greeneville as "comfortably predictable," it actually is ever-evolving, just like the girls.

With autumn comes the spooky season. When I think of my favorite Halloweens as a kid, my costumes are the most vivid memories. Like talented Leah in the series, my mom handmade our gorgeous costumes every year. As I sauntered around the neighborhood dressed as an iridescent Rainbow Brite (including yarn wig), a baker with accoutrements spilling out of my pockets, the Statue of Liberty carrying a torch, or Dorothy from *The Wizard of Oz* (where of course I had the glittery ruby slippers), the evening was all about impersonating my favorite fictional character. This same idea gave me the chance to dress Tessa up as the perfect Nancy Drew. Like my mom, accuracy was key to the final result. In preparation for *A Haunting in Greeneville*, I researched many *Nancy Drew* covers and consulted with an expert on the subject. What you see on the cover and described in the book is a compilation of different vintage Nancy-dresses over the years.

Despite my affinity for accuracy, ironically, my own costume that stands out above them all is one that no one could seem to guess correctly. It was a silky mint green gown with a collar, tie sash, and shimmery hem. On my head sat a sparkly, pearl tiara. And every time my sister (who was an easily identifiable pilgrim) and I rang a neighbor's doorbell and yelled "Trick or Treat!" the homeowner would declare, "What a lovely princess you are." I would hold my five-year-old head up high and scold them, announcing, "I'm not a princess. I'm a QUEEN!" The sentiment spoke volumes about who I was as a child. In my mind, why would anyone want the more simplistic job of a princess when she could rule the entire land? A queen has power and a kingdom. A princess only has a prince!

THE TOWN OF GREENEVILLE HEIGHTS

I'm often asked why I chose to set this series in the fictional town of Greeneville Heights, instead of a real location. Inspired by River Heights in *Nancy Drew* novels, Greeneville is the quintessential southern town where you know your neighbors, kids can safely ride their bikes all over town, and local businesses thrive under a sun-drenched blue sky. The most popular writing advice says to *write what you know.* Growing up, I moved around frequently and never really had a close connection to one city or town. Greeneville is that picture-perfect place where you wish you grew up and hope exists somewhere in reality. In fiction, the possibilities are endless, and I feel that is also true for Greeneville. In many ways, it could be said that Greeneville Heights is the most important character in *The Wright Detective* series.

TIDBITS ABOUT THE NOVEL

Like Tessa, I grew up around a treehouse, at least for part of my childhood. Unfortunately, it wasn't perched atop a majestic maple in my backyard. While we did have the sparkling pool, I had to venture across the street to my friend Jenny's house to mount her treehouse. With no photos to speak of, my memory is a tad fuzzy. I do recall a table inside, where we'd conduct meetings, and large windows with views of her wooded backyard.

Tessa's run-in with gnats on the cross-country course came about after one of my evening runs, where I was bombarded by swarms of little bugs. As I choked on dozens of them while stumbling home, I knew I had to include them in her trail adventures. I doubt there's a runner on the planet who hasn't swallowed a bug or two!

"Huntington Manor on Waverly"

I didn't realize I was writing a Halloween story until I dived headfirst into the idea of a creepy Victorian, aptly called Huntington Manor. The name appeared in my subconscious from a building on my alma mater Syracuse University's campus (which actually isn't too far from Waverly Avenue). We used a combination of several dilapidated homes in Syracuse, New York as inspiration for the facade on the novel's cover.

Acknowledgments

As I've said before, publishing a novel is never an easy task, especially with a tight timeline and seasonal release. I'm lucky to have some amazing individuals who keep me on track and go above and beyond to raise the bar with each book launch. Many thanks …

To EB, for being the first eyes to land on the final version. I hope this mystery lives up to the last and keeps you guessing! Your editorial comments made me smile, even on nights when I could barely keep my eyes open.

To Lane, for generously going through my first draft with a fine-tooth comb. I'm so glad you finally got that particular ending you've been patiently waiting for.

To my cover designer, Michael Borkowski, for an incredible fourth collaboration. A special thanks for creating the spookiest and most detailed cover yet and for fulfilling my dream of making Tessa the perfect Nancy Drew.

To Megan, for your love of timeless *Nancy Drew* stories, support for my neo-vintage series, and incomparable knowledge of all things *Nancy*.

To my Link Press Ambassadors, for enthusiastically sharing my work and my passion for "Bridging the Gap." When the days are long and my task list is even longer, you give me the energy to keep pushing our mission statement and the ideas to fulfill it.

To my talented mom, for spending tireless hours behind a sewing machine and creating such mind-blowing Halloween costumes. Who would have thought my vivid imagination would someday turn into a career as a published author? I definitely would never have guessed. I'm able to write Tessa's adventures because I can pull the ideas from such a fantastic childhood.

To Jonathan, for continuing to be my work's number-one fan and especially for designing an accurate Victorian haunted house to serve as Huntington Manor. Knowing you have my back through this publishing journey gives me the confidence to keep going.

About The Author

Kelly Swan Taylor is the author of the popular young adult novel *The Winning Ingredient* and the sleuthy middle grade series *The Wright Detective*. When she's not concocting unique recipes in her kitchen or hovering over her keyboard, this attorney and former laboratory scientist spends her time as a competitive runner. With experience racing from sun-drenched Hawaii to frigid Iceland, her first publishing credit was in Simon & Schuster's best-selling book series, *Chicken Soup for the Soul, Running for Good*, highlighting the historic 2013 and 2014 Boston Marathons. Growing up immersed in beloved "Teen" novels, Kelly now crafts her own sweet stories that bridge the gap between middle grade and young adult fiction that is so often forgotten but so sorely needed in the market today. In fact, she is so passionate about bridging this gap that she founded the imprint Link Press, dedicated to bringing these stories back to young readers. She has a soft spot for the kind and sincere yet flawed character, who tries to do the right thing, stumbles along the way, but eventually becomes a hero in everyday life. Kelly resides in Providence, Rhode Island with her architect husband, Jonathan, and her spirit animal and trusted kitty, Otto.

You can connect with Kelly on various social media platforms and subscribe to her newsletter via linktr.ee/KellySwanTaylor.

If you enjoyed *The Wright Detective*, please consider leaving a review on Amazon or Goodreads.

Keep reading for a sneak peek!
The Wright Detective
Book Four: A Charming Mystery

About Link Press

*The goal of Link Press is to bridge the gap
between middle grade and young adult fiction that
is so necessary in the marketplace but so often forgotten.*

With the aging up of young adult fiction over the past couple of decades, teen readers are increasingly being left out. Parents, teachers, librarians, and especially readers walk into bookstores and find they are wedged between two sections that are often too young or too old. To complicate matters, young readers tend to "read up." So, to the shock of parents, their 12-year-olds are stuck reading very adult stories with 17-year-old protagonists. Anyone can tell you, life is very different from the ages of 12 to 17.

Therefore, writers need to bridge that gap. But the publishing industry is just as confused as the readers. What do you do with a 13 or 14-year-old protagonist? Sadly, the current answer is nothing. Publishers are reluctant to print those stories. The simple suggestion is to change the age of the protagonist. The result is that the formative, all-important years between middle school and high school are obliterated in fiction just because an age range doesn't fit into a mold.

While writers of children's literature should always be encouraged to pen the stories that move them, tweens and teens should be part of that movement. At Link Press, young readers are always the primary focus.

As an author with this innovative press, Kelly Swan Taylor is passionate about filling that middle grade-young adult gap and bringing these stories back to the readers. Link Press believes there is an indelible connection between these reading age groups that forms a strong bond for strong storytelling.

Want to learn more about Link Press?

Visit authorklswantaylor.wixsite.com/home/link-press.

Book Four: Chapter 1

Tessa's sapphire eyes scanned the clay oval track, then shifted from her bare right ankle to the brace in her hand. She let out a long exhale, her breath creating a puff of smoke in the chilly February air. Track season was only weeks away, but as far as Tessa was concerned, a year away would be a better scenario. "Stop being a coward," she mumbled to herself as a smoke signal of frigid breath encircled her. Shaking off her apprehension, she discarded the brace on the track and attempted another lap—for the fourth time. But, like all her previous attempts, she wasn't far down the lane when her body seized up and slowed to a walk. "What is wrong with me?" Tessa grumbled as she rounded the track.

But she knew what was wrong, at least on the outside—her ankle injury was healed, but her head was not. No matter how hard she tried, every time the "track star" ran, the same fear crept up. Tessa's thoughts replayed her last cross-country meet in the fall, when she twisted her ankle in a deep mud pit along the course. Her pediatrician mom, as well as a specialist in sports medicine, said she was perfectly healthy to start running again. She only wished they'd tell that to her internal dialogue, which wouldn't seem to relent. Tessa was so embarrassed, she hadn't confided in anyone, including her best friend and teammate Riley. In fact, she had even resorted to fibbing whenever her bestie wanted to train together over the winter.

Deep guilt weighed her down as she trudged to the other end of the track. Tessa couldn't think of a single time she'd lied to her best friend, until now. As guilt turned into anger, she reached for her useless ankle brace once again and kicked it with all her might.

"Hey, nice kick! You trying out for the soccer team?" she heard from the entrance to the stadium. Looking up with a start, Tessa immediately recognized her boyfriend Mason approaching. He'd just recovered from an impressive duck, only narrowly missing a brace to his head. Partially embarrassed and mostly speechless, she watched him scoop up the brace from the edge of the track and hand it to her. "I thought you didn't need this anymore, right?"

Ignoring his question, she said, "Um, what brings you here?" when she finally found her voice.

"Just finished Saturday practice," he answered simply but with a dark brown eyebrow raised. He was obviously still wearing his basketball warm-ups and sneakers and carrying his duffel bag. "Playoffs, remember?"

Tessa let out an uncomfortable laugh. Of course, Greeneville Heights Middle's basketball team was once again preparing for an extended season, similar to last year's championship-winning one. Mason was the talented point guard and captain of the team. "Um, yeah. Sorry. Just freezer brain after, um, being out here so long ... running." *Or standing still.*

As he set his bag down, his emerald eyes searched hers for a beat, and he stepped closer for a tight hug. "You okay?"

Lowering her gaze to the track, she muttered, "Yup. Just peachy." She pulled away from their embrace and absently ran her fingers over the old gold charm bracelet dangling from her wrist.

"You've been wearing that a lot. Still hoping to solve that mystery?"

In addition to being an eighth-grade track star, Tessa was also the town's super sleuth, solving Greeneville Heights' most mind-bending mysteries from the cozy confines of her treehouse with her three best friends and the TSLR Detective Agency. A few months ago, she'd found the lovely heirloom inside the pocket of a dress from her favorite clothing store's vintage section. From that moment on, Tessa knew she had to get down to the bottom of that mystery and find its owner.

"There's something about it," she said, inspecting the many detailed charms dangling from the bracelet's chain. "Like it has a history that needs to be told, or at least remembered."

She looked up to Mason staring at her again, his face lighting up with a kind smile. "Well, the team has a bye week coming up. No Saturday practice. How about we finally head over to Carmichael's?" His grin turned whimsical. "I've missed our sleuthing adventures."

Tessa couldn't help but smile herself. Leave it to Mason to help her forget her troubles with a simple mention of her favorite activity. She'd wanted to visit the town's most respected jewelry store for a while and question, er, chat with one of its owners, premier craftsman Gene. "That sounds like fun."

"Come on. Let's get you out of the cold," Mason said, hooking his arm around her and leading them off the track.

She nodded, her gaze falling on the brace in her hand.

"So, think you could tell me what that was all about someday?" Mason asked, pointing to the brace.

Tessa suppressed a sigh, her eyes meeting his. "Yeah. Someday."

THE WINNING INGREDIENT

As the past and the present collide, one baker and one quarterback team up. The two might be the winning ingredient in a timeless recipe.

Tough cookie Mia DeSalvo can throw a perfect spiral and bake perfect biscotti. But, as George Washington High's top student and ninth-grade class president, she's thrown off her game when asked to tutor boarding school drop-out and star quarterback Bryce Fitzgerald. Despite his to-die-for dimples, he's a total bore. Besides, her plate is already full, trying to save her family's struggling century-old Italian bakery.

With the help of her Nonna Antoinette's Sicilian cookbook, Mia secretly devotes her free time to developing new recipes. But she isn't the only one with a secret. Once rumors start swirling around Bryce's lightning-speed exit from prestigious Chadwick Academy, she's determined to get to the bottom of it.

When Mia stumbles upon Bryce's beautifully written journal, it's clear his talents aren't confined to the football field. While the journal may hold all the answers she's looking for, the weight of its heartbreaking words may be too much for her to carry.

Armed with an antique cookbook and a football, this unlikely pair will discover the importance of embracing an enduring legacy and keeping cherished memories alive.